"You w...
what y...

She gro...
comes to this relationship stuff. I just asked you
to be my *friend* and ten minutes later I'm grilling
you about other women, making you think I'm
demanding exclusivity."

"But you do want exclusivity, don't you?" He had no
doubt that she did. "See, that's the thing, Tessa. You
have to tell me what you want."

She blew out her cheeks with a hard breath. "Well,
how about if you could be exclusive for the next two
weeks, anyway?"

Carson tried not to grin. "Even though we're just
friends?"

She covered her face with her hands. "We shouldn't
even be talking about this right now. It's too *early* to
be talking about this."

He suggested, "How about this? I promise not
to seduce any strange women for the next two
weeks—present company excluded."

She let her hands drop to her lap, revealing bright
spots of red high on her cheeks. "Maybe you
shouldn't warn me ahead that you'll be trying to
seduce me."

"Why not? We both know that I will, so the least I
can do is be honest about it."

MONTANA MAVERICKS: THE BABY BONANZA—
Meet Rust Creek Falls' newest bundles of joy!

Dear Reader,

Neither Tessa Strickland nor Carson Drake has time for love—or babies. But one night of forbidden passion is about to change their minds—and hearts—forever.

Carson Drake has been in Rust Creek Falls, Montana, for two weeks. He's trying to track down the small town's eccentric moonshine-maker, Homer Gilmore. Carson wants to bottle Homer's famous moonshine and sell it all over the world. But he can't even get a meeting with Homer. Carson's considering heading back home to Los Angeles. He's not a big fan of small towns, anyway. He loves the big-city life.

And then he meets Tessa.

Tessa Strickland has been there and done that with hot, dynamic alpha males like Carson Drake. She vows to stay away from him. Right now, she only wants a chance to live a settled, family-centered, happy life right there in Rust Creek Falls.

But the charming tycoon is irresistible. What can it hurt to spend a sunny holiday afternoon at his side? They'll enjoy each other's company and then he'll return to the big city while she remains in the small town she loves...

Happy reading everyone,

Christine Rimmer

Marriage, Maverick Style!

———

Christine Rimmer

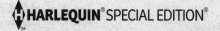

HARLEQUIN® SPECIAL EDITION®

Special thanks and acknowledgment to Christine Rimmer
for her contribution to the
Montana Mavericks: The Baby Bonanza continuity.

Recycling programs
for this product may
not exist in your area.

ISBN-13: 978-0-373-65967-8

Marriage, Maverick Style!

Copyright © 2016 by Harlequin Books S.A.

Printed in U.S.A.

Christine Rimmer came to her profession the long way around. She tried everything from acting to teaching to telephone sales. Now she's finally found work that suits her perfectly. She insists she never had a problem keeping a job—she was merely gaining "life experience" for her future as a novelist. Christine lives with her family in Oregon. Visit her at christinerimmer.com.

Books by Christine Rimmer

Harlequin Special Edition

The Bravos of Justice Creek

Carter Bravo's Christmas Bride
The Good Girl's Second Chance
Not Quite Married

The Bravo Royales

A Bravo Christmas Wedding
The Earl's Pregnant Bride
The Prince's Cinderella Bride
Holiday Royale
How to Marry a Princess
Her Highness and the Bodyguard
The Rancher's Christmas Princess

Bravo Family Ties

A Bravo Homecoming
Marriage, Bravo Style!
Donovan's Child
Expecting the Boss's Baby

Montana Mavericks: What Happened at the Wedding?

The Maverick's Accidental Bride

Montana Mavericks: 20 Years in the Saddle!

Million-Dollar Maverick

Visit the Author Profile page at Harlequin.com
for more titles.

For MSR,
always.

Chapter One

Carson Drake was ready to go home to LA.

As president and CEO of both Drake Distilleries and Drake Hospitality, Carson enjoyed luxury cars, willing, sophisticated women and very old Scotch, not necessarily in that order. As for small country towns where everybody knew everybody and every holiday included flag-waving and a parade?

Didn't thrill him in the least.

So what, really, was he doing here on the town hall steps in a tiny dot on the Montana map called Rust Creek Falls? Carson pondered that question as he watched the Rust Creek Falls Baby Bonanza Memorial Day Parade wander by. All around him flags waved. And there were babies. A whole bunch of babies.

Carson had nothing against babies. As long they belonged to someone else, babies were fine with him. But did he have any interest in watching a parade that *featured* babies?

The answer would be no.

Beside him, Ryan Roarke, a lawyer and Carson's friend of several years, said, "That's Emmet DePaulo." Ryan waved at a tall, thin older man on the Rust Creek Falls Medical Clinic float as it rolled by. The man was dressed in a white coat and had a stethoscope slung around his neck. "Emmet runs the local clinic with the help of Callie Crawford, who's—"

"Nate Crawford's wife, I remember," Carson finished for him. The Crawfords were one of the town's first families. Nate had a lot of influence in Rust Creek Falls, which meant he was someone Carson had made it a point to get to know.

Not that all the connections he'd forged in the past two weeks had done him much good, Carson thought glumly as he settled into a slouch against one of the pillars that flanked the steps. It had been a crazy idea, anyway. And he shouldn't let his lack of progress get him down. Not every gamble ended up in the win column. Sometimes a man simply had to accept that he was out of his element and going nowhere fast.

Carson was no quitter, but the plan wasn't happening. He needed to—

His mind went dead blank as he shoved off the pillar and snapped to his full height.

Who's that? he almost demanded of Ryan.

But he shut his mouth over the eager words and simply stared instead.

Damn. She was something. Just the sight of her had emptied his brain of rational thought and slammed all his senses straight into overload.

She rode one of the floats and was dressed as a stork.

Had anyone asked him a moment before if a woman in a stork costume could be hot, he would have laughed. But she *was* hot.

Her thick brown hair poked out from under the long orange stork bill, escaping the white fluffy stork hood to curl around her flushed cheeks. She was perched on a box covered in white cotton batting—to make it look like a cloud, he assumed. In her wings, she held a tiny squalling baby wrapped up in a blue blanket. Her slim legs, encased in orange tights, ended in platterlike webbed orange feet. She should have looked ridiculous—and she did.

Ridiculous. Adorable.

And hot.

Giant pink-and-blue letters sprinkled with glitter proclaimed the float "The Rust Creek Falls Gazette."

"That's Kayla, Kristen's twin," Ryan said, which made zero sense to Carson.

But then he ordered his brain to start working again and noticed the other woman standing beside his beautiful stork. Rigged out to look like the Statue of Liberty, holding her torch high and wearing a pageant-style sash that read, "The Rust Creek Rambler," Miss Liberty waved and smiled as the float drifted past. *She* was the one Ryan had just called Kayla. Carson deduced this because the woman with the torch was a double for Ryan's wife, Kristen.

Ryan kept talking. "Kayla is the recently outed mystery gossip columnist known as—"

"Judging by the sash, I'm thinking the Rust Creek Rambler?"

"Right. Kayla had us all fooled. No one suspected she could be the one who knew everyone's secrets and put them in the *Gazette*. Kayla's quiet, you know? She's the shy one. Nothing like my Kristen."

Carson tuned his friend out. The sweet stork with the wailing blue bundle had all his attention once again.

As he stared, she actually seemed to *feel* his gaze on her; her slim body went perfectly still. Then, slowly, she turned her white, billed head his way—and bam! Just like in some sappy, romantic movie, their eyes collided and locked. And damned if it didn't feel exactly as they always made it seem in the movies. As though she had reached out and touched him. As though they'd just shared a private, way-too-intimate conversation.

As if they were the only two people in the world.

He gaped, and she stared back at him with her sweet mouth hanging open, clearly oblivious in that moment to everything but him, though the band across the street played loudly and badly and some kid nearby had set off a chain of firecrackers and the baby in her arms continued to wail.

What was it about her?

Carson couldn't have said. Maybe it was those big, shining eyes, or that slightly frantic look on her incomparable face—a face that reminded him of his perfect girl-next-door fantasy *and* some bold gypsy woman, both at the same time. Maybe it was the stork costume. Most of the women he knew wouldn't be caught dead dressed as a stork.

But whatever it was about her that had him gaping like a lovesick fool, he *had* to meet her.

Her float rolled on past. Next came the Veterans of Foreign Wars float, with men and women in uniform holding babies in camo and waving way too many flags. As the band launched into "The Ballad of the Green Berets," Carson tried to figure out what had just happened to him.

Slowly, reality crept in—reality wrapped in a blue blanket and wailing.

The woman had a *baby*, for God's sake. Carson liked his women free and unencumbered. And there was not only the baby to consider but also the real possibility of a husband.

Was he losing his mind? He would never make a move on a woman with a baby. If she had a husband that would simply be wrong. And if she didn't, well, there would still be the baby. If he'd wanted kids, he wouldn't be divorced.

You'd think he'd been sampling the magic moonshine that had brought him to Montana in the first place, the magic moonshine created by a local eccentric named Homer Gilmore. Carson wanted the moonshine formula for Drake Distilleries. So far, he'd gotten nowhere near his admittedly out-there goal.

Which was why he'd just about convinced himself to give up and go home.

But the sight of the girl changed all that. The sight of the girl had him thinking that he didn't really want to give up. He just needed something to go right; that was all. He needed a win.

Meeting the adorable girl in the stork costume would definitely cheer him up, even with the damn baby—as long as there was no husband involved.

So then. First and foremost, he needed to find out if she was already taken.

At least that was easily done.

He asked Ryan, "Did you see the girl in the stork costume?"

Ryan gave it right up. "Tessa Strickland. Lives in Bozeman. She's visiting her grandparents at their boardinghouse."

Tessa. It suited her. "Married to…?"

Ryan shot Carson a narrow-eyed, you-can't-fool-a-lawyer look. "You're interested in Tessa. Why?"

"Ryan, is she married or not?"

His friend shoved back that shock of sable hair that was always falling over his forehead. "Tessa's single."

"But with a baby."

"You *are* interested."

"Would that somehow be a problem?"

Ryan smirked. "No problem at all. And Tessa's got no baby." *She's single, no baby.* Things were definitely looking up. Ryan added, "The baby is Kayla's—you remember, Kristen's sister, the Rust Creek Rambler in the Lady Liberty costume?"

Not that it really mattered but... "How do you know who that baby belongs to?"

"I will repeat, Tessa doesn't have a baby, whereas Kayla *is* married to Trey Strickland, and they have a son. Little Gilmore is just two months old. Kayla gave up her job writing the gossip column last year. She and Trey live down in Thunder Canyon now, but they come back to visit often. Somebody else writes the Rambler column now. Nobody knows who, but apparently someone talked Kayla into riding on the float. For old time's sake would be my guess."

"Props to you, man. You're here six months and you know everything about everyone."

Ryan extended both arms wide. "Welcome to my new hometown." Actually, Ryan and Kristen lived in nearby Kalispell, but why quibble over mere facts? And Ryan was smirking again. "The baby's named Gilmore. Get it?"

Carson stared at him, deadpan. "You're not serious."

"As a guilty verdict."

"They named their baby after Homer Gilmore?"

"Yes, they did."

"Who names their kid after a crazy old homeless guy?"

Ryan leaned closer and lowered his voice. "Kayla and Trey first got together last Fourth of July…" He arched a dark eyebrow as he let the sentence trail off.

Carson took his meaning. "You're telling me that they 'got together' over a glass of Homer's moonshine and in the biblical sense?"

"You said it—I didn't." The previous Fourth of July, a lot of women had drunk the famous moonshine, left their inhibitions behind and ended up pregnant—thus, the current Baby Bonanza. Ryan added, "As for why Tessa was holding Kayla's baby, I'm guessing that managing the torch *and* the baby was too much for Kayla, so she got Tessa to carry Gil—and you're definitely interested. Just admit it."

"I have another question."

"Carson. Admit it."

"Wait. Listen. Kayla's husband is a Strickland, you said, same as Tessa. So then, Trey Strickland must be Tessa's brother, right?"

"Wrong. Trey and Tessa are cousins and—Carson, what are you up to here? We've been friends a long time. I'm happy to introduce you around and tell you everything you need to know. But you've got to be up front with me. I *care* about what happens in this town. What do you want with Tessa?"

Carson met Ryan's eyes—and admitted the truth. "I think she's gorgeous, and I want to meet her. Is there something wrong with that?"

Ryan made a low, self-satisfied sound. "I knew it. Rust Creek Falls is getting under your skin."

"No, it's not."

"Yes, it is. You're just like the rest of us."

"Uh-uh."

"Oh, yeah. You'll fall in love with Tessa, and you'll never want to leave."

Carson had to make an effort not to scoff. "I just want to meet the girl. Can you make that happen?"

"Consider it done."

Tessa rocked the crying baby and ordered her racing heart to slow down.

But baby Gil kept right on bawling, and Tessa's heart kept beating way too fast and much too hard. Dear God, she was horrible with babies. They were so small and vulnerable and she always felt like she was holding them wrong. And boy, did little Gil have a set of lungs on him. How could someone so tiny make such a racket?

"Shh now, it's okay. Shh, sweetie, shh…" She tried to sound soothing as her heart galloped a mile a minute and a voice in her brain ordered her to toss the baby to his mother, leap right down off the moving float and run away from Main Street as fast as her webbed feet would carry her.

She really did need to get out of there. And she needed to do it ASAP, before *he* found her—and, no, she didn't know him. She'd never seen the man before in her life. She had no idea who he was or what he was doing in town.

What she did know, what she'd known at the first sight of him, was that he would be looking for her.

She had to make certain that he didn't find her. Because that man was nothing but trouble for someone like her.

Oh, yeah. One look at him and she knew it all.

Because he *had* it all. Tall, broad-shouldered and

killer-hot, he had dark, intense eyes and thick brown hair, chiseled cheekbones and a beautiful, soft, dangerous mouth. He'd looked like he owned the place—the steps he stood on, the town hall behind him, the whole of Rust Creek Falls and the valley and mountains around it.

Tessa could tell just from the perfect cut of his jacket and the proud set of those broad shoulders that he had money to burn.

Just the sight of him, just the way he'd looked at her...

Oh, she knew the kind of man he was, knew that look he gave her. That look was as dangerous as that beautiful mouth of his.

The last time she'd met a man who gave her that kind of look, she'd thrown away her job, her future, *everything*, to follow him—and ended up two years later running home to Bozeman to try to glue the shattered pieces of her life back together.

No way could she afford a disaster like that again.

Kayla glanced down at her. "You doing okay, Tessa?"

"Fine," she lied and rocked the howling Gil some more.

"Just hold on. We're almost there."

There was Rust Creek Falls Elementary School, where the parade had started and would end after a slow and stately procession up one side of Main Street and back down the other.

Why couldn't they hurry a little?

At this pace, he would probably be waiting for her, standing there in the parking lot, the sun picking up bronze highlights in his thick brown hair, looking like a dream come true when she knew very well he was really her worst nightmare just waiting to happen all over again.

Yes, she'd been instantly and powerfully attracted to

him. The look on that too-handsome face had said he felt the same. And that was the problem.

Tessa knew all too well where such powerful attractions led: to the complete destruction of the life she'd so painstakingly built for herself. She would not make that mistake twice. *Uh-uh. No way.*

Five minutes later—minutes that seemed like forever—they turned into the school parking lot. As soon as the float stopped rolling, Tessa jumped to her feet. Taking pity on her, Kayla set down her Lady Liberty torch and reached for the baby.

Gil stopped crying the second his mother's arms closed around him. "Thanks, Tessa." Kayla gave her a glowing, new-mommy smile.

Tessa was already jumping to the blacktop, headed for her battered mini-SUV on the far side of the lot. "No problem. Happy to help," she called back with a quick wave.

"We'll see you at the picnic," Kayla called after her.

Tessa waved again but didn't answer. She wouldn't be going to the Memorial Day picnic in the park, after all. *He* was far too likely to show up there, all ready to help her ruin her life for a second time.

She hurried on, grateful beyond measure that she'd thought to drive her car. It wasn't that far to her grandmother's boardinghouse, but her stupid webbed stork feet would have really slowed her down. Not to mention, she was far too noticeable dressed as a big white bird.

Yes, she realized it was absurd to imagine that the dark-eyed stranger with whom she'd exchanged a single heated glance might be coming to find her, might even now be on her trail, determined to run her to ground. Absurd, but still...

She knew he would be looking for her, knew it in the

shiver beneath her skin, the rapid tattoo of her pulse, the heated rush of her blood through her veins. She could taste it on her tongue with every shaky breath she drew.

It was ridiculous for her to think it, but she thought it, anyway. He *would* be coming after her.

And she needed to make sure he didn't find her. Getting to the safety of the boardinghouse was priority number one.

Main Street was packed with parade-goers, so she took North Broomtail Road. Tessa had her windows down. As she rolled along, she could smell the burning hickory wood from the big cast-iron smokers trucked to Rust Creek Falls Park before dawn. The giant racks of ribs and barbecue would have been slow-smoking all day long. The picnic in the park would go on for the rest of the day and into the night.

At Cedar Street she turned left. A minute later, she was pulling into the parking lot behind a ramshackle four-story Victorian—her grandmother's boardinghouse. Strickland's Boarding House was purple, or it used to be years ago. The color had slowly faded to lavender gray.

Tessa parked, jumped out and headed for the steps to the back porch, her ridiculous orange stork feet slapping the ground with each step. She didn't breathe easy until she was inside and on her way up the narrow back stairs.

In her room, she shut and locked the door and wiggled out of the stork suit. She felt sweaty and nervous and completely out of sorts, so she put on her robe, grabbed her toiletries caddy and went down the hall to the bathroom she shared with the tenant in the room next to hers. It was blessedly empty—the whole house felt empty and quiet. Everyone was probably celebrating on Main Street or over at the park.

She took her time, had a nice, soothing shower, slathered herself in lotion afterward and put real care into blowing her unruly curls into smooth, silky waves. She put on makeup, too—which didn't make a lot of sense if she planned to hide in her room for the rest of the day.

But that was the thing. By the time she got around to applying makeup, an hour had passed since she'd locked eyes with the stranger on Main Street. As the minutes ticked by, her panic and dread had faded down to a faint edginess mixed with a really annoying sense of anticipation.

Come on. He was just a guy—yeah, a really hot guy with beautiful, intense eyes and a mouth made for kissing. But just a guy, nonetheless. It was hardly a crime to be hot and rich and look kissable, now, was it?

She'd overreacted—that was all. And it was silly to let a shared glance with a stranger ruin her holiday. The more she considered the situation, the more determined she became not to run away from this guy.

She was not hiding in her room.

She was taking this out-of-nowhere attraction as a good sign, a sort of reawakening, an indication that she really had recovered—from the awful, depressing way it had ended with Miles *and* from the loss of the hard-earned, successful life that she'd so cavalierly thrown away to be with him.

Tessa returned to her room and dressed in a white tank that showed a little bit of tummy. She pulled on skinny jeans and her favorite red cowboy boots. She looked good, she thought. Confident. And relaxed.

On the way out the door, she grabbed her Peter Grimm straw cowboy hat with the studs and rhinestones, the leopard-print accents and the crimson cross overlay. The park was half a block from the boardinghouse, so she left her car in the boardinghouse lot and walked.

She was going to have a good time today, damn it. The past didn't own her. Not anymore.

A single shared glance during the parade didn't mean a thing. That man was a complete stranger, and he'd probably forgotten all about her by now.

Most likely, she'd never see the guy again.

Chapter Two

Tessa left the sidewalk and started across the rough park grass. She strode confidently toward the rows of coolers filled with ice and canned soft drinks.

Halfway there, Ryan Roarke caught her arm. "Tessa. Come on over here. There's someone I want you to meet."

She turned—and there *he* was, not twenty feet away under a cottonwood, with Kristen, Kayla and Trey. *He* stared right at her, a sinful look in those beautiful eyes and a smile playing at the corners of his too-tempting mouth. She half stumbled at the sight of him.

Ryan steadied her. "Whoa. You okay?"

She was. Absolutely. She was meeting Mr. Tall, Dark and Dangerous, and it would be fine. Because he was not Miles and now was not then. "Whoa is right. I think I stepped in a gopher hole."

Ryan, who was playful and smooth and a little bit

goofy all at the same time, gave her a knowing grin. "Gotta watch out for those."

"Tell me about it."

Ryan led her to the group under the cottonwood. She gave Kristen and Trey each a hug and touched Kayla's arm in greeting.

And then the moment came. *He* spoke to her. "Hello, Tessa." She lifted her chin and met those dark eyes— really, he was much too tall. Six-four, at least. Too tall, too hot, too…everything. She felt breathless all over again, felt that hungry shiver slide beneath her skin.

Ryan said, "Tessa, this is Carson Drake. He's up from LA on business. I've known him for years, used to do legal work for him now and then."

Tessa swallowed her breathlessness and teased, "Are you telling me he's harmless and I should trust him?"

Ryan hesitated. "Harmless. Hmm. Don't know if I'd go that far."

"Don't listen to him," the man himself cut in gruffly. Then he stage-whispered to Ryan, "You're supposed to be on my side, remember?"

"Well, I am on your side, man. I'm just not sure if *harmless* is the right word for you."

Kristen moved in close to her husband. She tipped her head up and pressed a kiss to Ryan's square jaw. "Sweetheart, Tessa's all grown up. She can handle Carson."

Tessa made a show of rolling her eyes. "Why am I feeling like I'm being set up here?"

"Because I asked to meet you." That deep, velvety voice rubbed along her nerve endings like an actual caress. Her stomach hollowed out as she stared into his eyes. The warning bells in her head started ringing again, loud and clear.

She ignored them. They were getting no power over

her. It was a beautiful day, and she meant to have fun. She looked straight at Carson again, took the full force of those dark eyes head-on. "So, Carson. What kind of business is it that brings you to Rust Creek Falls?"

Ryan volunteered, "He's here to try and make a deal with Homer Gilmore."

She kept looking at Carson. He stared right back at her. "What could Homer possibly have that you would want?"

"I want to talk to him about that famous moonshine of his."

"You want to buy some moonshine?"

"I want to buy the formula."

"Had any luck with that?"

"Not a lot. I've been here two weeks trying to set up a meeting with the man. It's not happening—though Homer *has* called me four times." Carson's brow furrowed. "At least, I think it was him. But then, I understand he's homeless. Does he even have a phone? And how did he get my cell number, anyway? Maybe someone's just pranking me." He sent Ryan a suspicious glance.

Ryan put up both hands. "Don't give me that look. If you've been pranked, it wasn't me."

Kayla suggested, "Homer always knows more than you'd think. He's a very bright man, and he has a big heart. He's just a little bit odd."

Tessa asked Carson, "So what did Homer—if it even *was* Homer—say when he called you?"

He gazed at her so steadily. A ripple of pleasure spread through her at the obvious admiration in his eyes. "Homer told me that he knew I was looking for him and he was 'working' on it."

"Working on what?"

Carson lifted a shoulder in a half shrug. "Your guess

is as good as mine. He said he *might* be willing to talk business with me. Soon."

Trey prompted, "And?"

"And that's it."

"He called you four times and that's all he said?" Kristen asked.

"Pretty much. It was discouraging. You'd think a homeless person would be eager to meet with someone who only wants to make him rich. Not Homer Gilmore, apparently."

"You're serious?" Tessa didn't really get it. "You want to buy Homer's moonshine formula and that's going to make him rich?"

"That's right." Carson reached out and took her hand. His touch sent warmth cascading through her. He pulled her closer—and she let him. "Come on. Let's get a drink." He wrapped her fingers around his arm. She felt the pricey fabric of his sport coat, the rock-hard muscles beneath, and she didn't know whether she was scared to death or exhilarated. Carson Drake was even more gorgeous and magnetic close up than from a distance. And he smelled amazing. He probably had his aftershave made specifically for him—bespoke, no doubt, from that famous perfumer in London, at a cost of thousands for a formula all his own.

And it was worth every penny, too.

He gave her a smile.

Pow! A lightning strike of wonderfulness, a hot blast of pure pleasure. It felt so good, to have this particular man looking at her as though there was no one else in the world—*too* good, and she knew it.

She'd been here before and she should get away. Fast.

But she did nothing of the sort. Instead, she said, "I'll have a drink with you—but only if you tell me more about how you're going to buy Homer's moonshine formula and then make him rich."

"Done."

They waved at the others and he led her to the row of coolers, where he grabbed a Budweiser and she took a ginger ale. Arm in arm, they wandered beneath the trees looking for a place to sit—and stopping to visit with just about everyone they passed. Two weeks he'd said he'd been in town. He certainly hadn't wasted any time getting to know people.

Eventually, they found a rough wooden bench at the foot of a giant fir tree. They sat down together, and Carson told her about his clubs and restaurants in Southern California and about Drake Distilleries.

"I know your products," she said. "High-end Scotch, rye and whiskey. Vodka and gin, too. And are you telling me you're hoping to bottle and sell Homer's moonshine in liquor stores all over the country?"

"All over the world, as a matter of fact."

"Wow."

"My family has been making good liquor for nearly a hundred years. When the story of the magic moonshine popped up on the wire services and the web, I read all about it. That was when it happened. I got the shiver."

"Which shiver is that?"

"The one I get when I have a great idea—like packaging Homer's moonshine for international distribution under the Drake label."

"Sounds a little crazy to me."

"Sometimes the best ideas are kind of crazy. I called Ryan. He gave me more details. Homer's famous formula is supposed to be delicious. I want to find out if it's as good as everyone seems to think—and if it is, I want it."

"Be careful," she warned. "Last Fourth of July, people drank Homer's moonshine and then did things they didn't even remember the next morning."

"I take my business seriously," he replied, his eyes level on hers. "And there are a lot of laws governing the bottling and distribution of alcoholic spirits. If I ever get my hands on Homer's formula, there will be extensive testing and trials before the finished product ever reaches the marketplace."

She tipped her head down and found herself staring at his boots. They were cowboy boots. Designer cowboy boots. The kind that cost as much as a used car. She sighed at the sight and lifted her gaze to him again. "It is kind of magical, what happened last year. I wasn't here, but everyone said people had the best time of their lives. There was a lot of hooking up."

"Thus, the Baby Bonanza."

"Exactly. People behaved way out of character, lost all control. Homer put the moonshine in the wedding punch, which was only supposed to have a small amount of sparkling wine in it. Nobody knew what they were drinking."

"I heard about that, too. The old fool is lucky nobody sued his ass."

"At first no one knew how the punch got spiked. For a while, there was talk about tracking down the culprit and putting him in jail. It was months before Homer confessed that he was the one."

"Was he ever arrested or even sued?"

"Nope. By then, folks were past wanting him to pay for what he'd done. It was getting to be something of a town legend, one of those stories people tell their kids, who turn around and tell *their* kids. It was as if Homer's moonshine allowed people to be…swept away, to do the things they would ordinarily only dream of doing. I mean, this little town is not the kind of place where people go to a wedding reception in the park and then wake up the next morning with a stranger, minus their clothes."

He leaned closer, so his forehead almost touched the brim of her hat, bringing the heat of his big body and the wonderful, subtle scent of his skin. "The whole aphrodisiac angle could be interesting—for marketing, I mean."

"Marketing." She put some effort into sounding less breathless and more sarcastic. "Because sex sells, right?"

"You said it—I didn't." His mouth was only inches from hers.

She thought about kissing him, and wanted that. Too much. To get a little distance, she brought up her hands and pushed lightly at his chest. "You're in my space."

One corner of that sinful mouth kicked up. "I think I like it in your space."

She kept her hands on that broad, hard chest, felt the strong, even beating of his heart—and slowly shook her head.

He took the hint, leaning back against the bench again and sipping his beer. "Ryan tells me you're from Bozeman."

"Born, bred and raised."

"You have a job there in Bozeman, Tessa?"

"I'm a graphic designer. I freelance with a small Bozeman firm—and I mean very small, so small the owner closes it down every summer."

"And that gives you a chance to have a nice, long visit in beautiful Rust Creek Falls every year?"

"Exactly. I also take work on my own. I have a website, StricklandGraphix.com—that's an *x* instead of a *cs*, in case you'd like to pay me a whole bunch of money to design your next marketing campaign."

"Are you good?"

"Now, how do you think I'm going to answer that?"

"Tell me you're terrific. I like a woman with confidence."

She took off her hat and dropped it on the bench between them. "Glad to hear it. Because when it comes to design, I know my stuff." *Even if I was blackballed from the industry and am highly unlikely to work in a major design firm or ad agency ever again.*

"Where did you study?"

"The School of Visual Arts."

"In New York?"

She poked him with her elbow. "Your look of complete surprise is not the least flattering."

"That's a great school." He said it with real admiration.

She shouldn't bask in his approval. But she did. "One of the best. I worked in New York for a while after I graduated."

"What brought you home to Bozeman?"

"Now, *that's* a long story. One you don't need to hear right this minute."

"But I would love to hear it." He was leaning close again, his arm along the back of the bench behind her, all manly and much too exciting. "You should tell me. Now." How did he do that? Have her longing to open her mouth and blather out every stupid mistake she'd ever made?

Uh-uh. Not happening. "But I'm not telling you now—so let it go."

"Maybe you'll tell me someday?" He sounded almost wistful, and that made her like him more, made her think that he was more than just some cocky rich guy, that there was at least a little vulnerability under the swagger.

"I guess anything's possible," she answered, keeping it vague, longing to move on from the uncomfortable subject.

Again, he retreated to his side of the bench. She drank

a sip of ginger ale. Finally, he said, "You looked amazing in that stork costume."

"Oh, please."

"You did. You looked dorky and sweet and intriguing and original."

"Dorky, huh?"

"Yeah. Dorky. And perfect. Almost as perfect as you look right now. I couldn't wait to meet you. And now I never want to leave your side."

"I'll bet."

He put up a hand as though swearing an oath. "Honest truth."

She let out a big, fake sigh. "Not so perfect with babies, unfortunately. Poor little Gil—that's Kayla and my cousin Trey's baby, the one I was holding during the parade."

"I remember."

"Did you hear him wailing?"

"I did. Yes."

"He's probably scarred for life after having *me* hold him for the whole parade."

"I'm not much of a baby person, either," Carson confessed with very little regret.

She teased, "So you're saying that we have something in common?"

"I'll bet we have a lot in common." He sounded way too sincere for her peace of mind. She tried to think of something light and easy to say in response, but she had nothing. He picked up her hat, tipped it back and forth so the rhinestone accents glittered in the sunlight, and then set it back down between them. "Any particular reason you rode the *Gazette*'s float?"

"Two reasons. One, I need work and I'm trying to get in good with the paper's editor and publisher. I love Rust Creek Falls and I'm considering moving here permanently—if I can pull enough business together from my website and locally to make ends meet, that is."

"And the second reason?"

She leaned closer and whispered in his ear, "The stork costume fit me."

He chuckled at that. Then he asked about her family. "Ryan told me that you're staying at your grandmother's boardinghouse."

She explained that she had two sisters, one of whom still lived in Bozeman, as did their mom and dad. "My other sister, Claire, her husband, Levi, and Bekka, their little girl, live here at the boardinghouse. Levi manages a furniture store in Kalispell and Claire is the boarding-house cook."

Carson listened to her ramble on. He really seemed to want to know everything about her. She found his interest flattering.

Maybe too flattering. Was she playing with fire?

Of course not. She'd met an interesting, attentive man, and she was enjoying his company.

Nothing wrong with that.

Eventually, they got up and each took a beer from the coolers. They visited with friends and family until the bar-becue came off the smokers; then they sat together at a pic-nic table with Ryan and Kristen, Trey and Kayla. Tessa's sister Claire and her husband, Levi, joined them, too.

Tessa was having a fabulous time.

Her original fears about Carson seemed so silly now. He *liked* her. *She* liked *him*.

It was a beautiful day, and she was spending it with a handsome, hunky guy. It would go nowhere, and she was happy with that. Before very long he would return to his glamorous life in LA. She would stay right here in

Rust Creek Falls, enjoying her summer break and trying to figure out what to do with the rest of her life.

Later, as twilight fell, she and Carson got a blanket from his car. They spread the blanket on the grass, got comfortable and talked some more.

She confessed that she was kind of at a crossroads, trying to decide where to take her graphic design career. There was her nice, safe job in Bozeman and the growing business she was building through her website. "I kind of want to try leaving the Bozeman job and focusing on freelancing independently, but it's tricky."

He stuck his long legs out in front of him and crossed them at the ankles. "I thought you said you wanted to move here, to Rust Creek Falls."

"I do, but that doesn't really fit with my ambitions for work. I'm slowly accepting that eventually I need to choose between trying again for a more ambitious career and a move here."

"Go big," he suggested.

"And what, exactly, does that mean?"

He shrugged. "You need to be where the action is. Why don't you move to LA?"

She set her hat on the blanket between them and stretched out on her back. Folding her hands on her stomach, she stared up at the darkening sky. "You weren't listening to me."

He leaned over her and touched her chin with a light brush of his finger, causing a bunch of small, winged creatures to take flight in her belly. "I would be there. To help you get settled."

She tried to keep it light. "Oh, I just bet you would."

"Can you dial back the sarcasm?" He held her eyes.

"Carson, you hardly know me."

"And that's my point. I want to know you better."

There was a moment—a long, sweet one—when he gazed down at her and she looked up at him. The world seemed wide-open at that moment, bright and so beautiful, bursting with hope and limitless possibility.

He whispered, "It's just a thought."

"Don't tempt me." She meant it to sound teasing. Flirtatious. But somehow, it came out too soft. Too full of yearning.

But then the band started playing over by the portable dance floor beneath the warm glow of the party lights strung between the trees.

"Come on." He took her hand and pulled her to her feet. "Let's dance."

And they did dance. For over an hour, they never left the floor. He was more than a foot taller than her, but when he wrapped his big arms around her, it felt only... right. He knew the two-step and how to line dance.

When she told him she hadn't expected an LA boy to know the cowboy dances, he laughed. "You oughta see my disco moves."

"Okay, Carson. Now you're starting to freak me out."

Eventually, they got bottles of water from the coolers and returned to the blanket. Theirs was a great spot, out of the way of the action, shadowed and private, with only the thick swirl of the stars and the waning moon overhead for light.

They whispered together like a couple of bad children plotting insurrections against unwary adults. He told her that he'd been married to his high school sweetheart, Marianne. "Marianne wanted to start a family right away."

"And you didn't want kids, right?"

"Right. I realized I'd married too young. We divorced.

She remarried a couple of years later. Her husband Greg's a great guy. They have four kids."

She stretched out on her back again and stared up at the stars. "So you're saying she's happy?"

"Very. I don't see much of her anymore, but it's good between us, you know? We're past all the ugly stuff. She ended up finding just what she wanted."

"And what about you?"

"I'm happy, too. I like my life. It's all worked out fine." He leaned over her, bending closer.

It just seemed so natural, so absolutely right, to offer her mouth to him, to welcome his kiss.

His lips settled over hers, light as a breath. They were every bit as soft and supple as they looked. She sighed in welcome as little prickles of pleasure danced through her, and she was glad, so glad, that she'd denied her silly fears and come to the park, after all. That she'd met this charming man and was sharing a great evening with him.

When he pulled back, his eyes were darker than ever. "What is it about you, Tessa? I can't take my eyes off you. I feel like I've known you forever. And how come you taste so good?"

She laughed. "Oh, you silver-tongued devil, you." She was trying to decide whether or not to kiss him again when a raspy throat-clearing sound came from a clump of bushes about ten feet away.

Tessa sat up. "What was that?"

Carson challenged, "Who's there?"

Branches rustled—and an old man emerged from right out of the center of a big bush. He wore baggy black jeans, a frayed rope for a belt, battered lace-up work boots and the dingy top half of a union suit as a shirt. Bristly gray whiskers peppered his wattled cheeks. What was left of his hair stood up at all angles.

Tessa recognized him instantly. "Homer Gilmore, were you eavesdropping on us?"

Chapter Three

Homer Gilmore blinked as though waking himself from a sound sleep—and then he grinned wide, showing crooked, yellowed teeth. "Well, if it ain't little Tessa Strickland. Stayin' at your grandma's place for the summer?"

"Yes, I am. And you didn't answer my question."

Homer scratched his stubbly cheek. "Me? Eavesdropping?" He put on a hurt expression. "Tessa, you know me better than that."

Beside her, Carson rose smoothly to his feet and held down a hand for her. She took it, and he pulled her up to stand beside him.

Homer came toward them.

Carson seemed bemused. "Homer Gilmore. Face-to-face at last."

Homer recognized him. "Carson Drake." He accepted Carson's offered hand and gave it a quick pump before letting go. "Told you I'd be in touch."

"So then, that really was you on the phone?"

"'Course it was." Homer had a mason jar of clear liquid in his left hand. "Here." He shoved it toward Carson.

Carson eyed the jar doubtfully. "What's this?"

"*This* is what you came here to get." Homer grabbed Carson's hand and slapped the jar into it.

"No kidding." Carson held the jar up toward the party lights in the distance. "Homer Gilmore's magic moonshine?"

"The one and only." Homer spoke proudly, puffing out his scrawny chest. "Truth is, I like your style, kid. And here's what I want you to do. Try a taste or two. See what you think. Then we can talk."

"I'm sorry." Carson actually did sound regretful. "It doesn't work that way." He tried to hand the jar back.

Homer refused to take it. "*I* say how it works. Taste it."

"Look, we need a meeting. A real meeting. Yes, there should be sampling, but formal sampling, in a professional setting. And chemical analysis, of course—but all that comes later. First, how about we meet for dinner and we can discuss—"

"Hold on." Homer put up a hand. "We'll get to the talk and the dang *analysis*. But first, you try it. This deal goes nowhere until you do."

"Homer, you're not listening to me. I can't just—"

"Nope. Stop. You heard what I said. Have yourself a taste. After that, we'll talk."

"When, exactly, will we talk?"

"Don't get pushy, kid. I'll be in touch."

Carson opened his mouth to say something else—but then shut it without saying anything. Tessa got that. What was the point? Homer wasn't listening. With a wink and a nod in her direction, the old man turned and walked away. Tessa and Carson stared after him as he vanished into the darkness of the trees.

Baffled, Carson stared down at the jar in his hand. "I don't believe this."

Tessa dropped to the blanket again. "It's Homer. What can you expect?"

"You think he might be crazy?"

"Of course not. He's a little peculiar, that's all. Being an oddball doesn't make you crazy. Kayla had it right. He really does have a good heart."

"If you say so." But he seemed far from convinced. She patted the space beside her. He folded his tall frame down next to her. "So…" He set the jar on the blanket next to her hat. For several seconds, they stared at it together. Over near the dance floor, the band launched into the next number.

Tessa laughed when she recognized the song. "That's 'Alcohol' by Brad Paisley. Perfect, huh?"

Carson slanted her a look full of mischief and delicious badness. "Want to try it?"

She *did* want to try it. She was really, really curious— just to know how it might taste, to maybe get a sense of whether or not any of the outrageous rumors about it might be true.

"Tessa?" he prompted when she failed to answer him.

She tried to remind herself of all the reasons that taking a chance on Homer's moonshine was not a good idea. "It could be dangerous…"

"You really think it's all that bad?"

"I didn't say bad. But you've heard the stories."

He flapped his arms. "Bok-bok-bok."

She laughed and gave his shoulder a playful shove. "Don't make chicken sounds at me. I'm being responsible."

He leaned a little closer. "And what fun is that?"

Oh, she did like him. She liked him a lot—liked him more and more the longer she was with him. He was not only hot. He was fun and smart and perceptive.

And a very good kisser.

Did he see in her eyes that she was thinking about kissing him? Seemed like he must have, because he leaned even closer and brushed a second kiss against her mouth.

So good.

His lips settled more firmly on hers. She sighed in pure delight and had to resist the sharp desire to slide a hand up around his neck and pull him closer still.

She was probably in big trouble.

But the more she got to know him, the less she feared her attraction to him and the more it just felt right to be sitting beside him under the stars with the band playing country favorites. The night had a glow about it, even here in the shadows on their private little square of blanket. She was having so much fun with him, loving every minute of this night. She never wanted it to end. She wanted to sit here and enjoy the man beside her and maybe, a little later, to get up and dance some more. And after that, to steal another kiss.

And another after that.

He reached for the mason jar and unscrewed the lid.

She leaned close and whispered, "You shouldn't have done that. It's all over now. Our lives will never be the same."

He arched an eyebrow at her. "The temptation is just too great. I can't resist." He sniffed at the open jar. "Smells like a peach." He tipped his head to the side, his expression suddenly far away. "I've always loved peaches."

"Peaches? No, really?"

"Really." He offered her the jar.

She took it and sniffed the contents for herself. "Hmm. Smells like summer."

"What'd I tell you?"

"But not peaches. Blackberries. Just a hint." She *really* wanted to taste it now. "I adore blackberries. They're my favorite fruit."

He wrapped his big hand over hers, and they held the jar together. He sniffed again, then insisted, "Admit it. It smells like peaches."

"No, Carson." She shook a finger at him. "Blackberries."

"Peaches."

"Blackberries. And look." She pulled the jar free of his grip and held it up to the party lights. "It even has a faint purple tint. Can't you see it?"

He took it from her hand and raised it high to decide for himself. "Looks more golden to me." He faked a serious expression. "And really, it *would* be a bad idea to taste it. Right?"

"Right. Bad idea to—Carson!" She let out a silly shriek as he took a careful sip from the jar. And then she leaned closer and asked, wide-eyed, "Well?"

He swallowed. Slowly. "That's good. Really good."

"Yeah?"

"Oh, yeah."

"Blackberries, right?" She nodded, holding his gaze, certain she could get him to nod along with her.

But his head went the other way—side to side. "Peaches. Definitely. And a hint of a moonshine burn going down. Gives it a nice kick."

"You're just playing with me."

He looked slightly wounded. "Never."

Only one way to make sure. "Give me that."

He held it away. "You'd better not. You never know what might happen."

"Knock it off, Carson. Hand it over."

"Whoa. Suddenly you're a tough girl."

"That's right. You don't want to mess with me."

"Never, ever would I mess with you." His voice was so smooth and manly, with just the perfect hint of roughness underneath. He gazed at her so solemnly. She really wanted to kiss him again.

Better not.

She reached for the moonshine instead. That time, he surrendered it. She put the jar to her lips and took a teeny, tiny sip.

Flavor bloomed on her tongue. A hint of sweet, summer fruit, and then wonderful heat going down. "Oh, yes. It's good."

"Told you so."

She gave a fist-pump. "Blackberry! Yes!" She sipped a little more, savoring the taste, relishing the lovely burn— and then handed it back to him.

A wonderful, sexy laugh escaped him. She laughed, too, the sound husky to her own ears.

He was watching her so closely, as though he couldn't get enough of just looking at her. She stared right back at him, a warm glow all through her. It was beautiful. Perfect.

She was lost in his eyes.

Chapter Four

Tessa woke slowly, smiling a little. All cozy and safe in bed, she was curled on her side, the blankets tucked up close under her chin.

But then she opened her eyes and felt her smile melt away.

What was this place?

The room was rustic, but richly so. She blinked and stared at an antique bronze mission-style glass lamp by the side of the bed. It sat on a night table made of gorgeous burled wood. Across the room—which was quite large—she saw a pair of French doors that looked out on a redwood deck with plush, padded furniture and a view of evergreen-blanketed mountains beyond. In the far distance, rugged snowcapped peaks poked the sky. It was clear, that sky, and very blue.

Daylight blue.

It must be morning.

But hadn't it been nighttime just a moment ago, nighttime at the Memorial Day picnic in Rust Creek Falls Park?

She shut her eyes and waited. Surely when she opened them again…

Nope. Nothing had changed. Same big, beautifully appointed room. Same morning light.

She pulled the covers tighter under her chin and whispered, "Where am I?" not really expecting an answer.

Then things got worse.

A sleepy male voice asked from behind her, "Tessa?"

She knew that voice—didn't she?

Carefully, slowly, clutching the covers close, she rolled to her back. With great reluctance, she turned her head. And there he was, Carson Drake, hair all rumpled, the scruff on his lean cheeks thicker than last night, his devastating mouth sexier than ever.

With a tiny squeal of distress, she lifted the covers enough to confirm her suspicions.

Yep.

Naked under there.

She grabbed the covers close again. "This cannot be happening."

He looked as bewildered as she felt. "Tessa, I don't…" Dark eyebrows drew together. Now he looked worried. About her. "Look, are you okay?"

She turned her gaze to the beautiful beamed ceiling above. Staring at it really hard, she whispered, "No, Carson. I am not okay." Panic rose. *Breathe.* She did, slowly, and exhaled with care. "I've…got nothing. I have no idea what we did for a least half of last night. I don't know how we got here." And then she went ahead and confessed the awful truth. "This is exactly like what everyone said happened to people last July Fourth. I've had a blackout,

I think. Last thing I remember, we were in the park sampling Homer's moonshine." She gulped and stared even harder at the ceiling overhead. "Do you, um, happen to know where we are and how we got here?"

"Hey. Look at me. Come on. Please?" He spoke so gently. As though her ears were tender and wounded—like her heart right now, like her self-respect and her very soul. She made herself face him again. He captured her gaze. "I didn't know—I promise you. I didn't believe that a jar of moonshine could really—"

"It's okay."

"No, it's not."

"Carson, what I mean is I didn't believe it, either. Just…would you answer my question, please? Where are we and how did we get here?"

"We're in my suite at Maverick Manor. But as to how we got here, I don't have a clue. I remember we drank the moonshine. And there are…flashes of memory after that. Us laughing on the blanket, staring up at the stars. I kissed you. And we danced."

"That was earlier."

"Yeah, and then we danced again, later. And…well, it all starts to go hazy after that."

"But did we…?" It seemed silly to even ask the question. They were here, together, naked. Almost certainly, they *had*.

He reached out a bare, beautifully muscled arm and scooped some bits of foil off the nightstand. "Looks like it."

"What do you mean?"

He opened those long fingers to reveal three empty condom wrappers. They crackled on his palm as the foil relaxed.

"Omigod." How could she? She didn't even *know* this

man. And yet here she was naked in bed with him, staring at empty condom wrappers with no recollection of using them. It was awful and embarrassing and not the kind of thing she would ever do—well, except with Miles. She'd fallen straight into bed with Miles the night she met him, too. But at least she was conscious when she did it. At least it had been her choice, and she'd loved every minute of it.

This, on the other hand…

No. Just…no.

This was all wrong. She didn't remember making a choice. She couldn't recall anything after those first few sips of moonshine.

Okay, she'd been attracted to him from the instant her eyes met his. Wildly so. But falling into bed with him? *Uh-uh. No way.*

"God. Tessa. Your face is dead white. Are you sure you're all right?" He was watching her as though he feared she might shatter.

Well, she wouldn't. Not a chance. She was tougher than that. Yeah, she'd messed up royally. But that didn't mean she couldn't hold it together. She let out a shaky little sigh. "I just can't believe that this is happening, that's all."

"At least we were safe about it," he offered sheepishly.

She played along, because she was not going to lose it right here in front of him. "Yeah. I guess that's something, right?"

"Right." He pushed himself to a sitting position.

She did the same, careful as she scooted up against the headboard to keep the blankets close. They leaned against the headboard side by side. She stared hard at the far wall and wished that the floor would just open up beneath her and swallow her whole.

The silence, weighted so heavily with regret and embarrassment, went on forever.

Finally, she murmured shakily, "I want to go home."

He looked at her again then. His eyes were so sad. "Tessa, I'm so sorry…"

She showed him the hand and aimed her chin high. "Don't. It's no more your fault than mine. I don't blame you. I drank that moonshine of my own free will." It had tasted so good. And she'd never really believed the stories about it. Until now. Slow fury rose in her. "I might have to kill Homer Gilmore, though." She spoke through clenched teeth. "Seriously. It's like we were roofied."

He made a low sound of agreement. "So much for my big plans to get the formula for Drake Distilleries. That stuff is way too dangerous."

She pressed a hand to her queasy stomach. "I may never drink anything with alcohol in it again."

"Believe me, I understand."

They shared a wry, weary glance, and she said, "I really do want to go now."

"All right."

She looked away, toward the balcony and the snow-capped mountains in the distance. The covers shifted as he left the bed. More fabric rustled.

He said, "I'll just use the bathroom." Footsteps padded away.

As soon as she heard the bathroom door close, she jumped from the bed, grabbed her wrinkled clothes from the bedside chair and put them on. Once she was fully dressed, including her socks and red boots, she went looking for her hat.

She found it on the coffee table in the sitting room—next to a sketch pad and a bunch of pastels and colored pencils. "What in the...?" She picked up the pad and turned the pages slowly.

The drawings were her own, though she had zero memory of creating them. And as to where she got the pad and pencils, who knew? But apparently, not only did she and Carson use three condoms last night; she'd also whipped him up an ad campaign for Homer's magic moonshine.

For the first time that morning, she almost smiled.

Not bad. Not bad at all. Clean, clear, imaginative and well executed, if she did say so herself. Even her domineering, tough-as-nails former boss, the legendary Della Storm of Innovation Media in New York, would approve. Tessa especially liked her rendering of a frosty-blue bottle with a sliver of silver moon on it and the words *Blue Muse* in a retro font. She also thought the sketch of a golden bottle with a lightning strike on the front was really good. That one was called *Peach Lightning* in bold copperplate Gothic. And the way she'd managed to work the Drake Distilleries logo of a rearing dragon into both designs? *Damn good.*

Glancing up from the pad in her hand, she stared into the middle distance, remembering how much fun she and Carson had had in the park, how they'd bantered back and forth over whether the 'shine was blackberry or peach. She'd loved every moment with Carson yesterday—at least, every moment that she could recall.

She heard the bathroom door open. With a hard sigh, she tossed the sketchbook back on the low table.

He appeared in the doorway to the bedroom, fully dressed in jeans, a knit shirt and a different pair of high-priced boots than he'd worn the day before. Dear Lord, he was a fine-looking man. Regret dragged at her heart that there couldn't be more between them.

But no. It had all gotten way too complicated too fast. She didn't need complications with a man, not until she had her own life figured out. She needed him to take her back to her grandmother's boardinghouse. After that, she never wanted to see that amazing face of his again.

Across the room, he stared her somberly. Probably trying to think of something to say to her.

She knew exactly how he felt. "I'll just use the bathroom and then I'm ready to go."

Carson found his car in his usual space in the parking lot. He'd had his keys in yesterday's jeans, so he must have driven them there. It freaked him the hell out to think that he'd gotten behind the wheel so drunk on moonshine he had no memory of the trip.

The ride back to town was a silent one.

Carson despised himself the whole way. And he couldn't stop thinking about the condom wrappers, couldn't stop asking himself if they were fools to depend on those empty wrappers as proof that they'd played it safe.

When he pulled in at the curb in front of the boardinghouse, she grabbed her hat off the seat with one hand and the door handle with the other. He should just let her go. It was obvious she wanted to get as far away from him as possible.

But he couldn't let her walk away. Not yet. First, they needed to deal with the consequences of their actions—whatever the hell those actions had actually been.

"Wait, Tessa. Please." She froze and stared at him, her dark hair a wild tangle of curls around her unforgettable gypsy-girl face. He made himself ask, "Are you on any kind of contraception?"

She winced and then confessed bleakly, "No. I had an

implant, but when it expired last time, I didn't replace it. And... I know, I know. Way more information than you needed."

His gut twisted at her news, but he kept his voice gentle and low. "I'm sorry, but I can't stop thinking that those condom wrappers don't really prove we were as careful as we needed to be." For that, he got a soft, unhappy groan.

She put her face in her hands. "You're right. You're absolutely right." With a ragged intake of breath, she lifted her head and squared her shoulders. "Don't worry about it. I'll take care of it. I'll get the morning-after pill today."

Rust Creek Falls had one general store. That store had no pharmacy area that he could remember. "Can you get it at Crawford's?"

She chuckled, a sound with very little humor in it. "No. I'll drive over to Kalispell. It's a quick trip, not a big deal."

He didn't want her doing that all alone. "I'll take you. We can go right now."

She looked at him for a long count of five. And then she answered firmly, "No, thank you. I appreciate the offer. You're a stand-up guy. But I really need to get through the rest of this walk of shame on my own." She grabbed the door handle again and was out on the sidewalk before he could think of some way to change her mind. "Goodbye, Carson," she said. The word had all the finality of a death sentence. She shut the door.

He watched her climb the boardinghouse steps and knew that it was over between them—over without really even getting started.

Tessa's grandmother Melba Strickland was waiting for her in the foyer just inside the front door.

"There you are." Melba reached out her long arms for

a hug. Tessa went into them. Her grandmother always smelled of homey, comforting things. Right now it was coffee and cinnamon toast and a faintly floral perfume. "When you didn't come down for breakfast at seven as usual, I got a little worried. I knocked on your door. No answer. I tried calling you, but your phone went straight to voice mail."

"Sorry." She'd left her phone in her room the night before. Because she'd only been running down the street to the park and she'd expected to return within a few hours. It must have died.

Her grandmother took her by the shoulders. "Are you all right?"

"I'm fine." Tessa resisted the urge to make up a lie that explained her whereabouts last night. Yes, her grandmother had old-fashioned values and wouldn't approve if Tessa said where she'd really been. But Tessa was a grown woman and her mistakes were her own to work out. Her grandma didn't need to hear it. "I want to grab a shower. Then I need to drive into Kalispell and pick up a few things." *You know, like the morning-after pill. Because I'm an idiot, but I'm trying to be a responsible one.*

Melba searched her face. "I just want you to know that I'm ready to listen anytime you need to talk."

Tessa's empty stomach hollowed further with a mixture of equal parts love and guilt. "I do know, Grandma. And I'm grateful."

Melba gave her shoulders a squeeze. "You need to eat."

"I really want to get going."

"Humor me. An egg, some toast, a nice cup of hot coffee…"

So Tessa followed Melba to the kitchen, where eighteen-month-old Bekka sat in a booster seat at the table, drinking from her favorite sippy cup and munching on Cheerios and grapes. It was after nine, so Levi was off at work in Kalispell.

"Auntie Tess, Auntie Tess! Kiss!" Bekka made loud smacking sounds until Tessa bent close and let the little girl press her plump, sticky lips to her cheek. Tessa might not be good with most babies, but at least her niece seemed to like her well enough. Bekka offered a fistful of Cheerios.

They were limp and soggy. Tessa ate one anyway as Bekka beamed her approval.

Then Tessa got herself some coffee, pausing to pat her sister's shoulder as she went by. Claire sent her a questioning look, and Tessa gave a rueful shrug in response. She set herself a place at the table, and Claire whipped her up some scrambled eggs. The food helped. Tessa felt a little better about it all once she'd eaten.

Upstairs, she hung her hat on the peg by the door, had a shower and paid no attention to the mild tenderness between her legs. She ignored the love bite on her left breast. It would fade to nothing in a day or two. She let the water run down over her, soothing her shaky nerves. And she tried not to regret what she couldn't even remember.

Not too much later, dressed in a short denim skirt and a soft plaid shirt, she was on her way to Kalispell. At the first drugstore she came to, she bought a root beer and the hormone pill she needed. She took the pill the moment she got back behind the wheel, sipping the root beer slowly as she drove back to town.

That taken care of, she helped Claire in the kitchen for a while and then went upstairs to check email and dig into some projects she'd acquired through her website. Last Friday, when she'd agreed to ride the *Gazette* float, she'd told Dawson Landry, the paper's editor and publisher, that she was looking for design work. Dawson had said that if she came by, he would put her to work. She'd said she would, on Tuesday.

Well, it was Tuesday. And follow-through mattered.

So once she'd made sure she was on top of her other projects, she called Dawson. He said to come on over.

At the *Gazette*, she spent a couple of hours punching up the layout for the next edition. Once she got absorbed in the work, she was glad she'd come. It helped to keep busy.

As for Carson, well, whatever they'd done last night, it wouldn't be happening again. Last night was clear proof that she should have followed her first instinct when it came to him, should have stayed at the boardinghouse and out of his way.

She wouldn't be seeing him anymore. She would get past her own stupid choices yet again. Everybody made mistakes and life went on.

And if Homer Gilmore knew what was good for him, he'd keep the hell away from her for the next hundred years.

Carson didn't notice the sketchbook until late that afternoon.

He'd driven into Kalispell, too. He'd had a late breakfast at a diner he found. And then he'd wandered around the downtown area, checking things out, seeing what the larger town had to offer.

Was he hoping he might run into Tessa?

A little. Maybe.

But it didn't happen.

It was so strange, the way he felt about her. He missed her. A lot. He'd met her less than twenty-four hour ago, yet somehow he felt as though he knew her. She had a kind of glow about her, an energy and warmth. Already he missed that glow.

His world was dimmer, less vibrant, without her.

As he drove back toward Rust Creek Falls, he realized that he hadn't felt this way about a woman in years. Not since he was fifteen and fell head over heels for Marianne.

He wished he could remember making love with Tessa. Somehow, even though he couldn't remember what they'd done late in the night, the clean, sweet scent of her skin and the lush texture of her hair were imprinted on his brain.

At the Manor, he spent a couple of hours catching up with email and messages. He got on the phone to a number of employees and associates in Southern California. When asked how the moonshine project was going, he said that it had fallen through.

He didn't, however, mention flying back to LA, though he might as well pack up and go. There was no reason to stay. So far, though, he'd failed to start filling suitcases. Nor had he alerted the pilot on standby in Kalispell to file a flight plan and get his plane ready to go.

At a little after four, Carson dropped to the sofa in the suite's sitting room and reached for the TV remote on the coffee table in front of him.

He noticed the two dozen colored pencils and bright, fat, chalklike pastels first. For several seconds, he frowned at them, wondering where they might have come from. Then he saw the sketchbook. The maids had been in and placed it just so on top of the complimentary stack of magazines.

Tessa. The sketchbook must be hers. But he didn't remember her carrying any art supplies with her yesterday. Where had the pad, the pencils and the pastels come from?

He had no idea. It was yet another lost piece of last night. Curious and way too eager to see what might be inside, he grabbed the sketch pad and started thumbing through it.

Instantly, at the first drawing of a series of different-shaped jars and bottles, he was impressed. Each design was unique. The jars were mason-style, the kind with raised lettering manufactured into the glass. Each one made him feel that he could reach out and grab it, that he could trace the pretty curves of the lettering with the pad of a finger. She had great skill with light and shadow, so the bottles almost seemed to have dimension, to be smooth and rounded, made of real glass.

Carson got that shiver—the one that happened whenever he had a really good idea.

These drawings of Tessa's gave him ideas.

She gave him ideas. Because beyond being gorgeous and original, with all that wild, dark hair and a husky laugh he couldn't get out of his head, Tessa Strickland had real talent. He slowly turned the pages, loving what he saw.

She knew how to communicate a concept; her execution was brilliant. Unfortunately, now that a deal with Homer was off the table, he wouldn't be able to use what she'd come up with here.

But you never knew. Homer Gilmore didn't have the moonshine market cornered. If Drake Distilleries developed their own, less dangerous brand of 'shine, the *Blue Muse* and *Peach Lightning* flavors might well have a future, after all.

And even if he gave up on making moonshine completely, Drake Distilleries could benefit from a talent like

Tessa's. And so could his restaurants and nightclubs. Targeted, carefully executed advertising and effective promotion were a lot of what made everything he put his name on successful. Adding Tessa to the firm that promoted his brand could work for him in a big way.

And for her, too. Before last night faded into oblivion, they had talked about her career, about where she might be going with it. He'd said she should go big. Now that he'd seen her work, he knew he'd been right. If he could make her a tempting enough offer, maybe he could convince her to come to LA, after all.

All at once he felt vindicated. He hadn't told his people he was returning to Southern California because he *wasn't*. Not yet.

Not until he'd convinced Tessa Strickland to move to LA, where he could help her have the kind of successful design career she so richly deserved. He knew he could give her a big boost professionally.

And if it went somewhere personal, too, he would be more than fine with that.

First thing the next morning, Carson called Jason Velasco, his contact at Interactive Marketing International in Century City. He was about to explain that he'd found a brilliant graphic designer and he was hoping she might be a fit for IMI. He planned to tell Jason that he wanted Tessa working on the various ad campaigns that IMI developed for both Drake Distilleries and Drake Hospitality, which was the mother company for Carson's clubs and restaurants.

But then he caught himself.

True, Jason knew where his bread was buttered. If Carson wanted Tessa working at IMI, Jason would damn well do all in his power to make that happen.

But how would Tessa react to Carson's setting her up for an interview without consulting her first?

Quite possibly not well.

Given that she'd walked away from him yesterday without a backward glance, he really couldn't afford to take the chance of pissing her off in any way.

And Jason was still waiting on the line, probably wondering if he'd hung up. Carson said lamely, "Hey! Just thought I'd call and check in, see how we're doing with the new campaign." Drake Distilleries was preparing to launch a series of flavored brandy-based liqueurs.

Jason gave him a quick rundown. Then he asked, "So you're still in the wilds of Montana on that supersecret new acquisition of yours?"

"Still in Montana, yes. And the project did start out as a secret. But this is a small town, and it's hard to keep a secret around here." He explained about Homer's moonshine, and how he'd thought it might work for Drake Distilleries. "But it was a long shot and it didn't pan out. The downstroke is it's a no go."

"That's too bad."

"Can't win 'em all."

"So you'll be on your way back now?"

"Not yet. I have a few more things I need to look into here first." *Things like how to convince a certain adorable brunette that California is the place for her.*

"But we'll see you on the twentieth?" On the twentieth, Jason and his team would be presenting the game plan for the liqueur campaign. It was an important meeting. In fact, Carson had more than one meeting he couldn't miss during that week. He would have to return to LA by then.

That gave him two and a half weeks to get through to Tessa. Ordinarily he had limitless confidence in his powers of persuasion. Not so much in this case.

"Carson? You still with me?"

"Right here. And of course I'll be there on the twentieth."

Once he hung up with Jason, Carson called Strickland's Boarding House. Tessa's sister Claire answered, politely identifying herself. He almost told her who he was. But then he remembered the look on Tessa's face when she'd left him the morning before. If Tessa knew he was calling, would she even come to the phone?

He decided to take no chances. "I'd like to speak with Tessa Strickland."

"Hold on."

A moment later, she came on the line. "This is Tessa."

Just the sound of her voice made his chest feel tight. He wanted to see her, wanted it a lot. "You probably won't believe this, but I can't stop thinking about you."

A silence. Not a welcoming one. "Hello, Carson."

"I was thinking maybe lunch. We could drive over to—"

"Carson, I don't think so."

He lowered his head and stared at his boots. "It's just lunch."

She spoke again, her voice almost a whisper. "Please don't worry. I went to Kalispell yesterday and took care of it."

"It?" And then he caught on. He swore low. "Come on, Tessa. Don't. I'm not calling about the damn morning-after pill."

A silence on her end. A long, gruesome one. Then finally, "It's just…not a good time for me to get anything started, you know?"

"Fine." Though it wasn't. Not fine in the least. "This isn't a personal call, anyway." That was only half a lie. He wanted to get close to her, absolutely. But he also wanted to help her have the career she deserved. "Did you know you left sketches in my suite?"

"Yeah. I saw the sketch pad on the coffee table and looked through it. I don't remember how or when it happened, but apparently we plotted out a moonshine campaign." She paused, then, "Wait a minute. You're going ahead with the moonshine thing after all?" Now she sounded surprised—and not in a good away.

"No."

She sighed. "Glad to hear it. You had me worried there for a minute."

"This isn't about the moonshine. It's about you, about your future. Those sketches are amazing. I want you to think about—"

"Carson."

He stared at his boots some more and knew he was getting nowhere. Feeling desperate and pitiful—emotions with which he'd never been the least familiar—he took one more stab at getting through to her. "You have so much talent. I only want to—"

"No, thank you," she said softly, with utter finality. "I have to go now. Goodbye."

Chapter Five

Tessa hung up the phone and hated herself.

She wanted to see Carson so much she could taste it, like a burning sensation on her tongue. She'd hurt him, blowing him off like that. She didn't want to hurt him.

She just...

She needed to keep her head about her, needed to remember that getting swept off her feet by a killer-handsome, charismatic rich guy didn't work for her.

Been there, done that. Not going there again.

She wanted *real* now—a down-to-earth life in this beautiful little town full of people she cared about. And if she couldn't make that happen here, she would come up with a workable compromise, one wherein she could build a satisfying career and still visit Rust Creek Falls at least a few times a year. Eventually, once she figured out how to make the life she wanted for herself, she might even start looking for a guy who wanted the same things she did.

Carson Drake was not that guy. And it really was for the best that she'd told him goodbye.

At first, after Tessa hung up on him, Carson was seriously pissed off. He spent half the day on the phone, keeping up with things in LA, asking himself constantly why he hadn't packed his bags and called his pilot.

That evening, he went downstairs to the hotel bar for a drink and ran into Nate Crawford, the owner of Maverick Manor. Nate said his wife, Callie, was working late at the medical clinic. "And I've been here at the hotel all day. How about a change of scenery? Follow me into town. We'll grab a beer at the Ace in the Hole." The no-frills saloon was the only bar inside the town limits.

At the Ace in the Hole, Carson had a longneck, played a little pool and talked business with Nate, who was always promoting investment opportunities in Rust Creek Falls. Nate wanted him to meet with some guy named Walker Jones who owned a number of day care centers all over the western states and was apparently on track to open a new day care in town—to cope with the recent baby boom, Carson assumed. Nate said Walker Jones might be willing to take on a silent partner or two.

"I'm in liquor and hospitality," Carson reminded the other man. "I know nothing about child care centers."

Nate shrugged. "Why not just meet with the guy? He'll be in town in a couple of weeks."

Carson should have said that he would be long gone by then. But he didn't.

Because he was going nowhere—not until he absolutely had to. Not until he'd found a way to get Tessa to spend a little more time with him, not until he'd gotten his chance to make her see that LA was the right move for her. He really had a thing for her. And he just couldn't walk away from that. Not until he was certain that it was never going anywhere.

Yeah, it didn't make a lot of sense. He'd spent the last decade carefully avoiding anything remotely resembling an actual relationship with a woman and he'd planned on keeping it that way.

But then there was Tessa. Just the sight of her in her silly stork costume, looking like she'd rather be anywhere else than on that float holding Kayla's baby…

One look at her and he'd known his plans were about to change.

He said, "I have meetings I can't miss in LA the week of the twentieth. But if your guy is here before then, sure. Let's have a drink at the Manor Bar, the three of us."

Nate set down his beer. "I'll let you know. Meanwhile, I've been meaning to ask…"

"Yeah?"

"Whatever happened with Homer Gilmore and that moonshine project of yours? You ever get him to meet with you?"

"I spoke with him briefly Monday night at the picnic."

Nate chuckled. "That Homer. One of a kind. And judging by the look on your face, the moonshine project is on hold?"

"You could say that."

"Don't want to talk about it, huh?"

"You could say that, too."

Nate got off his stool and clapped Carson on the shoulder. "Gotta tell you, Carson, I'm not surprised. Callie and I had a little of that wedding punch spiked by Homer last Fourth of July. I'm talking one small paper cupful each. It was a wild night for us—and that's just what I can remember of it."

"I hear you—believe me."

Nate looked at him sideways. "You did try it, then?"

"Yeah, I tried it. And I've learned my lesson. Homer's moonshine is powerful stuff. Drake Distilleries has no plans to unleash it on an unsuspecting world."

"I suppose that's wise." Nate stepped back to take his leave. "I need to head home. Callie should be done at the clinic by now." His green eyes gleamed with eagerness. The man couldn't wait to get home to his wife.

Carson felt a hot little stab of envy. He was eager, too. He wanted to see Tessa again, to watch her smile, hear her voice, brush a quick kiss against her wide mouth.

But that wasn't happening.

Not tonight, anyway.

The next morning, he admitted to himself that he needed help. He called Ryan.

"What's up?" Ryan demanded.

Carson cleared his throat. "I have a question."

"I'm here for you, man."

"Say, just for instance, that I wanted to get to know Tessa Strickland better…"

Ryan played along. "Okay, let's say you do."

"But Tessa's a little…reluctant." *Okay, fine.* She was a *lot* reluctant, but Ryan didn't need to know that.

"A woman actually capable of resisting *the* Carson Drake? Never been born."

Carson rubbed his temple where a headache was forming. He'd been on the phone for less than a minute and already he regretted making this call. "I need help, smartass, and you're giving me attitude."

"Really gone on her, huh? That was quick. Damn near instantaneous, as a matter of fact. But I'm not surprised."

"I swear to you, Ryan, if you start in about how I'm

destined to fall in love because this is Rust Creek Falls and that is what people do here, I will hang up on you."

"Go right ahead, man. And who will you ask for help next?"

Carson swore. "Very funny."

"Well, *I* kind of thought so—but okay. I've tortured you enough for one phone call. What do you need?"

"Ways to get closer to Tessa."

"You're turning stalker on me now?"

"I thought you said you were finished torturing me."

"That's not torture. That's just messing with your head."

"Ryan. Are you going to help me or not?"

Ryan heaved a big, hard sigh. "I suppose I have no choice. You're a victim of love, and you really need me."

He was so eager to get on with the conversation, he didn't even bother to argue about Ryan's indiscriminate use of the L word. "Terrific. Let's move forward. Got any suggestions?"

"Melba," said Ryan.

"Come again?"

"Melba Strickland, Tessa's grandmother? Owns the boardinghouse where Tessa is staying?"

"I remember. What about Melba Strickland?"

"You need to get friendly with her. You need to salt the old cow to get to the calf."

"What is that you just said?"

"It's an old country saying."

"Right. Because you're so damn country now."

"You put out a salt lick for the cow," Ryan patiently explained, "and her calf comes with her and then you can catch the calf—for whatever purpose. Tick removal. Branding…"

"How am I going to get friendly with Tessa's grandmother?"

"How do you get friendly with anyone? You get an introduction. Or you go to the places where they hang out."

"Like...?"

"Somehow you imagine I know where to look for Melba Strickland?"

"Well, this *is* your idea."

"Look. It's a really small town. Try the places everybody goes. Church, for instance."

"That's not till Sunday. It's Thursday."

"Carson Drake, you're a very impatient man. I think there's some kind of Bible study class at the community church tonight, as a matter of fact."

Bible study. Was he up for that? He supposed he would have to be. "Are you sure Melba will be there?"

"No. It was just a suggestion of somewhere she might possibly go. Let's see. What about Crawford's? Everyone goes to the general store at some point during the week."

"You want me to lurk around Crawford's General Store?"

"I'm assuming you'll be subtle about it." Ryan made a thoughtful sound. "There's the library. But I have no idea how often Melba goes there, if ever. Plus, a library is not the place to strike up a conversation. You're supposed to be quiet there... Let me think. Where else? Maybe the donut shop or Wings to Go. But I think church or Crawford's is a better bet for Melba. She's a busy older woman without a lot of time to waste munching donuts in coffee shops."

"What do I do once I actually figure out a way to meet the woman?"

"I already told you. You charm her. You make friends

with her, and she invites you home and Tessa will be there."

"I have to say, Ryan. This is about the weakest idea you've ever come up with."

"Sorry. That's all I've got for you. You need to spend some time coming up with your own ideas. And you need *not* to be in such a hurry."

"I live in Malibu. I have two corporations to run. I can't stay here forever."

"See, now? That's your problem. The women, as a rule, just fall in your lap. You're not used to having to work for something you want."

"I work damn hard, thank you."

"You know very well I'm not talking about business here. I'm talking about romance. I'm talking about—"

"Do. Not. Say. That. Word."

"I wouldn't dream of it. Now, get to work on Melba. And try to remember, Carson. This will be good for you. This will be character building."

Carson hung up from the call with Ryan and realized that he had no idea what Melba Strickland even looked like. He picked up his phone again to call Ryan back— and then set it back down. Hard.

He'd had more than enough of Ryan's advice for one day. He would find Melba Strickland on his own, thank you. How hard could that be?

Too hard, he realized in no time at all.

At first, he thought maybe he would just try asking a few people. Like Nate. Or maybe the mayor, Collin Traub. Or the sheriff, Gage Christensen. But the more he considered that approach, the more truly weird he realized he was going to sound. Because, seriously, what possible interest could a guy like him believably have in the elderly lady who ran the boardinghouse?

When he tried to picture himself explaining to Gage or Nate or Collin that he wanted to get to know Melba so he could get closer to Tessa Strickland...well, how was that going to look? Men in Rust Creek Falls were protective of women. He would come off as just what Ryan had jokingly called him: a stalker.

Ryan had suggested he try the library. He could go there and look through old copies of the *Rust Creek Falls Gazette.* Maybe he'd find a mention of Melba, hopefully with a photograph included.

But okay, say he got lucky with a nice, clear headshot of Tessa's grandmother to go by? Then what? It could take days of churchgoing and donut eating and lurking at the general store before he would even catch his first glimpse of the woman.

He didn't have days to waste. He had to be in LA on the twentieth, for God's sake. He needed to get things going with Tessa right away in order to have the next two weeks to convince her to give LA a shot.

Damn Ryan. He was no help at all.

Carson flopped back onto the sofa in his sitting room and scowled at the ceiling, mentally calling his longtime friend a whole bunch of bad names—and right then, just like that, the solution popped into his head.

Just like that, it all became crystal clear.

He knew what to do, and it was priceless.

A half an hour later, he marched up the front steps of Strickland's Boarding House and knocked on the door.

An old man in baggy trousers and a plaid shirt answered. "Howdy."

"I'm Carson Drake, in town on business."

The old guy took his offered hand and gave it a pump. "I'm Gene Strickland. Folks call me Old Gene." He ran a wrinkled hand over what was left of his hair and then moved back. "Come in, come in." Carson stepped over the threshold into a dark, old-fashioned entry hall with stairs rising up in the center of it. Old Gene shut the door. "You're that liquor fella, aren't you? The one trying to bottle Homer Gilmore's 'shine?"

Was there anyone in this town who didn't know more about his business than he did? He doubted it. "I'm the one."

"How's that workin' out for you?"

"Not well."

The old guy let out a cackle. "Why am I not surprised? What brings you to Strickland's?"

"I'm hoping you have a room available."

The wrinkles in Old Gene's forehead got even deeper. "I thought I heard you were stayin' out there at Maverick Manor with all the other rich folks?"

"I have been staying at the Manor, yes. But I've decided I would rather be here on Cedar Street, right in the thick of things." *And closer to Tessa*, he thought but didn't say.

"And that's gonna help you how?" Gene had very sharp eyes, and they were trained hard on Carson.

Carson almost asked the old coot what business it was of his. But he had a feeling that wouldn't go well for him. He punted for all he was worth. "I really like this town. And I've got about two more weeks here before I return to the rat race in LA. I want to…immerse myself in the real Rust Creek Falls experience, and that's not going to happen out at Maverick Manor."

More cackling from Old Gene. "*Immerse* yourself, huh?"

Carson gave a half shrug. "Hey. I'm from LA. We're big into immersion."

"Oh, I'll just bet." Old Gene gave him a long, measuring look. Then, finally, "Well, you'd better come on back to the office and I'll get my better half, Melba. She handles check-in."

Five minutes later, Carson stood at a check-in window in the boardinghouse office at the back of the building. He turned at the sound of footsteps. A sturdy-looking old woman in a button-front dress and sensible black shoes came through the door to the central hallway. She introduced herself. "Hello, I'm Melba, Gene's wife." His first thought—beyond how brilliantly he'd handled this—was that neither she nor her husband looked at all like Tessa. But then Melba smiled—a warm, wide smile.

Maybe there was a similarity, after all.

"Excuse me, young man."

He stepped aside, and Melba opened the door with the check-in window in it and entered the office cubicle on the other side. "Now," she said with another echo-of-Tessa smile. "I have a nice room on the third floor that has just come vacant. It's next to my granddaughter Tessa's room, as a matter of fact." Melba gave him a look from under her eyelashes, and he was absolutely certain she knew *everything* about Monday night—which, come to think of it, would be a hell of a lot more than *he* knew. She asked, "How's that sound?"

He opened his mouth, and the truth popped right out. "Just about perfect." Could he really be getting this lucky?

"You and Tessa will have to share a bath. All the rooms do. Gene says you're from LA and you were staying at the Manor before. You really don't mind sharing a bathroom?"

He kept his face harmlessly blank. "I'm sure it will be fine." And he whipped out his platinum card before she could tell him she'd changed her mind and she didn't want him anywhere near her granddaughter.

Melba ran the card through one of those ancient credit card sliders and then passed him his receipt, rattling off meal and snack options as she did it. Next, she reached to the side and grabbed something--a white plastic caddy--which she plunked on the office check-in window ledge in front of her. "You'll need this to carry your shampoo and shaving gear to and from the bathroom. Here's your key."

He couldn't quell his wide grin as he took the key and grabbed the white caddy. "Thank you."

She eyed him with what seemed to be vague suspicion. "Any questions?"

Now that he thought about it, he did have a question. "Do you have Wi-Fi?"

Melba made a disapproving sound, as though she thought internet access was just pure foolishness. "Gene likes his internet, my grandchildren say they have to have it when they come to visit and most folks these days can't get along without it. We do have it now, though service can be a bit spotty."

Spotty. Not good. But he would keep his suite at the Manor and stay in electronic communication with LA from there.

Melba gave him a small white card. "Here's the password."

"Terrific."

"Enjoy your stay."

"I'm sure I will."

Tessa sat in Emmet DePaulo's cramped office at the Rust Creek Falls Medical Clinic.

Emmet, a nurse practitioner who'd been running the

clinic for as long as Tessa could remember, held out his hand across the desk to her. Tessa rose to shake it. Emmet said, "We really appreciate this, Tessa. It's just me, Callie and Dawn." Callie Crawford was also a nurse practitioner. "Thank the good Lord for Callie. And Dawn. She's a lifesaver." An RN, Dawn Laramie had recently joined the clinic staff. "With all the babies born in the last few months, we need a pediatrician and we need one yesterday."

Tessa shut her laptop and tucked it under her arm. "I'll work up the material we talked about and email it to you tomorrow for approval." She would create a few eye-catching ads as well as simple text-only listings using the information Emmet had just given her. Once Emmet approved her work, she would place the ads for him online in medical forums and on job sites where doctors and nurses looked for employment. "You'll have that new doctor you need in no time."

Emmet came around the desk and walked her out to the waiting area, where every chair was taken. Babies were crying and Brandy, the clinic receptionist, looked about at the end of her rope. Tessa felt really good to be able to help in a good cause. Plus, due a lot to Callie Crawford's husband, Nate, who had plenty of money and put a fair amount of it into worthy causes, the clinic was well funded. Tessa would actually get paid for creating and placing the ads. Win-win in a big way.

Outside, it was cool and sunny. A gorgeous day. Tessa paused before ducking into her trusty Honda CR-V. She turned her face toward the mountains—and thought of Carson with a sharp little stab of what could only be called longing.

She'd been thinking of Carson a lot, way too much, really, since yesterday morning when she'd made it painfully clear to him that this thing between them was over. *Goodbye*, she'd told him. And that should have been the end of it.

Except for how her mind wouldn't stop turning back around to wondering about him and what he might be doing now. Except for the ache in her solar plexus that kept reminding her she missed him.

It was absurd. How could you miss a guy you hardly knew?

Yanking open her door, she dropped her shoulder bag and laptop on the passenger seat and slid in behind the wheel. She hauled the door shut—and then, with a sad little groan, sagged forward until her forehead met the wheel.

Okay, she kind of wished she'd given him more of a chance. Yeah, he was cocky and too rich and too good-looking, totally dangerous to her poor heart and her emotional equilibrium.

Still, she liked him. A lot. She loved being with him. And what could it hurt to enjoy his company for the few more days he might be in town? Just because he reminded her too much of Miles—well, how was that *his* fault?

And as for the craziness that had happened with the moonshine? Again, as she'd reminded herself more than once already, not Carson's fault. She'd drunk that stuff of her own free will—and he'd been just as knocked out by it as she had.

And then she'd freaked and blown it with him. *Way to go, Strickland.*

There was something…not really right about her. She was socially stunted, and she probably ought to get help. She felt powerfully drawn to Carson. She wanted to get to know him better—and so what had she done about that?

Told him to get lost. *Ugh.*

She longed to call him back and tell him she'd been all wrong to end things before they even really got started. She wanted to ask him for another chance.

Not that she would do that.

No. Better to accept her own idiocy, leave bad enough alone and try to do better next time.

A sad little laugh escaped her. Yeah, because killer-handsome, cocky guys who made her laugh, knew the two-step, thought her work was brilliant and turned her knees to jelly were so easy to come by.

Tessa lifted her forehead off the steering wheel, squared her shoulders and muttered, "Get over it," to the empty car.

He was probably long gone back to LA by now, anyway. She needed to let it go.

She started up the car and drove to the boarding-house—where she found Carson's rented Cadillac SUV parked in the lot behind the building.

Chapter Six

Carson had just finished hanging his shirts in the closet and putting his underwear in the ancient bowfront bureau when the tap came on the door. He shoved the drawer shut, tossed his empty suitcase in the closet and went to answer, hoping that just maybe it might be Tessa.

Score.

She looked amazing, eyes wide and somber, mouth twisted ruefully, standing right in front of him on the threadbare runner in the narrow hallway. She wore a soft pink shirt, black jeans with rolled cuffs and high-heeled sandals with ties that wrapped around her slim ankles. Her hair was loose, corkscrew curls wild and thick around that gypsy face. Just the sight of her raised his blood pressure and hollowed him out down low. He had to order his hungry arms not to reach for her.

"Tessa," he said prayerfully. "At last."

She cleared her throat, a thoroughly enchanting, nervous little sound. "I saw your car in the lot. When I went looking for you downstairs, my grandma shared the big news that you had taken the empty room next to mine…" Her voice trailed off. They stared at each other. Finally, she spoke again. "We should talk."

He stepped back, clearing the doorway.

When she entered, he shut the door and enjoyed the view as she walked to the bed and sat down on the bright red, white and blue quilt. When she patted the space beside her, he couldn't get over there fast enough.

He dropped down next to her and sucked in a slow breath through his nose. She smelled like a rose. A rose and some wonderful, sweet spice.

"What are you doing here?" Her words demanded answers, yet her eyes were soft.

He wanted to touch her, to brush her arm, take her hand. But he didn't dare. "I couldn't give up. Sorry. It's just not in me. Ryan suggested that I make friends with your grandmother."

She blinked in surprise. "My grandmother? What for?"

"As a way to get close to you."

She pondered that for a moment. Then, "That's a little…"

"Out there?" he volunteered when she seemed to have trouble coming up with the right words.

"Yeah."

"Well, Ryan's always been a little out there. But I had nothing, so I went with his suggestion. I was knocking myself out trying to come up with ways to become BFFs with your grandmother. And then I thought of just taking a room here." She looked at him so steadily, he could see gold flecks in those coffee-brown eyes of hers. And dear God, that mouth. He couldn't wait to kiss her again.

She sent a quick glance around the room. "Kind of a step down from Maverick Manor—wouldn't you say?"

"No way. I love it here. This is a terrific room. It has everything I need. A bed, a dresser. A bathroom down the hall…"

"I am making an effort *not* to roll my eyes."

He *had* to ask. "So does your grandmother know you spent Monday night with me? I swear, while I was talking to her, I got the feeling she knew it all."

Tessa actually chuckled. The sound warmed him through and through. "Let's play it smart and never ask her what she knows."

"Because she's one of those old ladies who doesn't believe in hot, sexy times outside of marriage?"

Tessa laughed again, a snorting little burst of sound that had him feeling downright hopeful about his chances with her, after all. "Actually, I don't think my grandma believes in hot, sexy times under any circumstances. But you never know. Did you meet my grandpa, too?"

"I did. And as you can see, I lived to tell about it."

"And Claire?"

"I haven't seen her yet. But I remember you mentioned that she lives here, too."

"There are two full apartments downstairs. My grandparents have one. My sister and her family have the other."

"And Claire and Levi have a little girl, right?"

"Yeah. Bekka. I love Bekka. She's the only baby who ever liked me." Her beautiful smile trembled a little. She lowered her gaze.

He resisted the urge to tip up her chin and make her meet his eyes again. "So you're not mad at me for moving in here?"

And then she did look at him. *God.* He wished she

would never look away. "No, Carson. I'm not mad. How long are you staying?"

"Till the nineteenth. I have meetings in LA the week of the twentieth."

She touched him then, just a quick brush of her hand on the bare skin of his forearm. Heat curled inside him, and he could have sworn that actual sparks flashed from the point of contact. Then she confessed, her voice barely a whisper, "I regretted saying goodbye to you almost from the moment I hung up the phone yesterday."

"Good." The word sounded rough to his own ears. "Because I'm going nowhere for the next two weeks."

She slanted him a sideways glance. "You mean that I'm getting a second chance with you whether I want one or not?"

All possible answers seemed dangerous. He settled on, "Yes."

"I…um. I want to take it slow, Carson. I want to…" She glanced down—and then up to meet his eyes full-on again. "Don't laugh."

He banished the smile that was trying to pull at his mouth. "I'm not laughing."

"I want to be friends with you. Friends first. And then we'll see."

Friends. Not really what he was going for. He wanted so much more. He wanted it all—everything that happened Monday night that he couldn't remember. He wanted her naked, pressed tight against him. Wanted to coil that wild, dark hair around his hand, kiss her breathless, bury himself to the hilt in that tight, pretty body of hers, make her beg him to go deeper, hear her cry out his name.

But none of that was happening right now. So he said

the only thing he could say, given the circumstances. "However you want it, Tessa."

"You're sure about that?"

"I am."

"Because, I'm…" She ran out of steam. Or maybe courage.

And that time he did reach out to curl a finger beneath her chin. She resisted at first, but then she gave in and lifted her gaze to his once more. He asked, "You're what?"

"I'm not good at this, you know?" She stared at him, her mouth soft and pliant, all earnestness, so sweetly sincere. "I'm kind of a doofus when it comes to romance and all that."

He laughed at that, though she'd warned him not to. "A doofus? No way, not you."

"Yes, me. Growing up, I wasn't even interested in boys."

Damn. He wanted to kiss her. Instead, he wrapped an arm around her and pulled her in snugly against his side. She didn't resist—on the contrary, she laid her head on his shoulder. He took total advantage and pressed a quick kiss into the dark cloud of her hair. "Not interested in boys?" he teased. "That can't be normal."

She nudged him with her shoulder. "You're just asking for trouble." But then she settled close again and continued. "I was obsessed, but not with boys. All I cared about was art. I was a total nerd about it. I spent hours drawing every day, and I never slacked on my schoolwork. I needed straight As so I could go to the best design school on scholarship. I got what I was after, a full ride to the college of my choice. I moved to New York, and I never looked back."

"But then, somehow, you ended up back in Bozeman?"

Several seconds ticked by before she answered. "Really, it's a long story and not all that interesting."

"That's pretty much what you said Monday night. And then you clammed up. But now that we've decided we're going to be friends, I think it's only fair that you go ahead and tell me."

"Oh, right. Because you're all about what's fair."

"Come on," he coaxed. "Tell me."

She tipped her head and looked up at him, her dark eyes turned darker, her mouth softer, more vulnerable. "Carson, I..."

"I really do want to know."

She rested her head on his shoulder once more. And finally, she confessed, "I messed up."

"Messed up how?"

"You're not going to give up, are you?" she grumbled. "Not until you know it all."

He smiled to himself. "No, I'm not. You might as well just tell me everything—get it over with so that we can move on."

"You're impossible."

"I've been called worse, believe me. So, you got a full scholarship to the School of Visual Arts and..."

She hesitated, but then she forged ahead with it. "I did well there. In my last year of college, I got a great internship with a small Brooklyn firm. Two months later, they gave me a real job. And I was hired away from them by *the* Della Storm, who is as close to legendary as anyone gets in the world of graphic design."

Carson stroked her hair, loving the feel of it, so thick and wild and warm. He coiled a few strands around his finger as she explained that Della Storm was not only a legend in her field but also tough, uncompromising and difficult to work for. At the age of twenty-four, Tessa had already been given a lot of responsibility and creative say in the projects she took on under Della's supervision. But then she met Della's ex-boyfriend, an archeologist named Miles Rutherford.

"It was insane, how fast I fell for him," Tessa said. "One look in those blue eyes of his, and I was just gone. In the space of a glance, I went from zero interest in love and romance to head over heels."

Already, Carson hated this Miles character, though for all he knew, the guy hadn't done a thing but be the man Tessa fell in love with. "Lucky Miles Rutherford. Let me guess. You were inseparable from that moment on."

"Pretty much."

"Tell me more about him."

She lifted her head from his shoulder. "Do we really need to go into all the gory details?"

He wanted to know everything about her—including the difficult stuff she was reluctant to share. "Come on. Just tell me."

"What can I say? He was from a wealthy Montana family and I felt this instant connection with him."

"How did you meet him?"

"It was one of those big charity events at the Waldorf, the women in full evening dress, the men looking sharp in black tie. We struck up a conversation and talked for hours—about Montana, about design, about Miles's life traveling the world. Then we went to his place and I stayed the night. I moved in with him the next day." She glanced up and scanned his face as though looking for clues as to what he might be thinking. "Go ahead. Say it."

He gave a half shrug. "That was quick."

"I know. And I knew it then, that it was all happening much too fast. But I didn't even care. From the first moment I saw him, he was everything to me. After that first night, I didn't care about my job, didn't give a damn about the career I'd spent my whole life up to that point building. I got sloppy. We were working on an important project, and Della trusted me to run it. I just blew the whole thing off. I messed up everything I'd worked so hard for. I let a lot of people down. It really was all on me. I chose some guy I didn't even know over my life and my responsibilities."

"You said that this Miles was your boss's ex?"

She shifted against him with a tiny sigh. "Caught that, did you?"

He kissed her hair again. "Not a lot gets by me."

"I'll bet. Yeah, Miles was Della's ex. He was completely over her."

"But *she* wasn't over *him*."

"Shh. This is *my* story."

"Am I right?"

"Yes, you are. Della wasn't over him. And I never had the guts to tell her that he and I were together. She found out about Miles and me around the same time I blew up that project she'd trusted me to run. She was furious with me on so many levels. She had no claim on Miles. But she did have every right to come after me for going AWOL on the job. She fired me and she promised me that she would see to it I never worked in a major firm again."

Carson thought about IMI. *The* Della Storm and her jealous vendetta aside, Tessa would have a job at IMI if he wanted her there—well, she would if he could talk her into going to work for them. "How long ago was it that this Storm woman fired you?"

"Four years. And when Della blackballed me, I have to tell you, I didn't even care. All I cared about was Miles. After that, I didn't pick up a sketchbook or open a graphic design program for a year and a half. I was with Miles, and that was plenty for me. He worked in South America, in Egypt and in Spain. When he wasn't on a dig, we lived in luxury in hotels in Paris, London, Rome, Marrakech—you name it. At first, it was like a fairy tale, but over time, the magic began to fade."

"How long were you with him?"

"Two years."

"Why did you break up?"

"He got over me, just like he got over Della before me. I'm pretty sure he was cheating on me before the end. And I was...well, I was starting to admit to myself that what we had wasn't really working for me, either. That I needed my *own* life, you know? I regretted tossing my career in the crapper like that. And then one day I walked in on Miles in bed with two gorgeous women, identical twins."

"Whoa."

"Exactly. That was a real eye-opener. I will never forget what he said to me. 'Darling. Join us.' He was smiling like it was nothing, daring me to make a scene."

"And you...?"

"I didn't say a word. I knew exactly what he was trying to tell me. He was done with me. I turned and left the room. Then I packed my stuff and flew home to Bozeman. The really sad part is, by then, I didn't even care. Seeing him with those two women was just the final nail in the coffin of our bad romance. I'd screwed up my life for some guy I didn't really even know."

"And I...remind you of him, of Miles?"

She eased free of his hold and scooted away a little. He wanted to pull her back but thought better of it. "I love Montana, Carson. I missed Montana during the years I was in New York. And then, with Miles, living from one hotel to the next, I missed home even more."

"Tessa." He waited until she looked at him. "Do I remind you of Miles?"

"You really, truly want me to answer that?"

He didn't, not really. But he needed to know. "Yes."

"Fine." She threw up both hands and then let them drop. "The more I'm around you, the less you remind me of him, the more you're just…you. But yeah. When I first saw you, standing on the town hall steps looking like you ruled the world, it was pretty much Miles all over again."

He got up, went to the window and stared out over the street below. When he faced her again, he made his position very clear. "I don't cheat. Yeah, I wanted to be free when my marriage ended. But I never got near another woman until I had my divorce."

"But there have been a *lot* of other women, right?"

"Is that somehow a crime?"

"Now who's not answering the question, Carson?"

He knew he was busted. "Okay. Yeah. There have been a lot of women. But I'm not seeing anyone now." Truthfully, in the past year or so, he'd started to feel edgy and dissatisfied again, just as he had when his marriage was ending. He'd had his years of freedom, and it had been a great ride. But spending his nights with a series of beautiful women he would never really know—didn't even want to know—just wasn't as exciting as it used to be.

Tessa prodded, "You sure there's no part-time girlfriend thinking she means more to you than she does?"

"Absolutely not."

"No good-time girls waiting at your Beverly Hills mansion for you to return and join them in the hot tub?"

"No. I live in Malibu, and I live alone."

She glared at him intently for a long count of five, as though if she only looked hard enough, she might see inside his skull and know with certainty his level of truthfulness. Finally, she nodded. "Okay, then," she said on a soft little sigh.

He had more questions—about a thousand of them. "Were you and Miles ever married?"

"No."

"But you were exclusive with him?"

"I thought so. But I thought a lot of things, and you see how well that turned out for me."

"You want *us* to be exclusive? That *is* what you're talking about here, right?"

She groaned at that. "See? I'm a mess when it comes to this relationship stuff. I just asked you to be my friend, and ten minutes later I'm grilling you about other women, making you think I'm demanding exclusivity."

"But you do want exclusivity, don't you?" He had no doubt that she did. "See, that's the thing, Tessa. You have to tell me what you want."

She blew out her cheeks with a hard breath. "Well, how about if you could be exclusive for the next two weeks, anyway?"

He tried not to grin. "Even though we're just friends?"

She covered her face with her hands. "We shouldn't even be talking about this right now. It's too early to be talking about this."

He suggested, "How about this? I promise not to seduce any strange women for the next two weeks—present company excluded."

She let her hands drop to her lap, revealing bright spots of red high on her cheeks. "Maybe you shouldn't warn me ahead of time that you'll be trying to seduce me."

"Why not? We both know that I will, so the least I can do is be honest about it."

"Hmm. Well, okay. I'm all for honesty." Her soft mouth

was trying not to smile. "And I admit that I *am* a little strange."

"But in a thoroughly captivating way."

She bent her dark head again and said almost shyly, "Every now and then, you say just the right thing."

"Tessa?"

"What?"

"Look at me." He waited until she met his eyes directly before asking, "Are you absolutely determined to stay in Montana? You wouldn't consider LA, even if you could get your dream job there?"

She hitched up that firm chin. "You're pushing too fast."

"I'm going home in two weeks."

"So then, could you maybe wait a few days at least before trying to talk me into moving to California when I've just said I want to be here? Besides, didn't you hear me say I was blackballed from my own industry?"

"With the right connections, anything is possible."

Her wide mouth tightened. "You mean *your* connections."

"That is exactly what I mean. You know IMI?"

She actually gaped. "You're telling me you think you can get me a job as a graphic designer with Interactive Marketing International?"

"I don't think it. I *know* it. And a *real* job, one that makes full use of your talent, one that's exciting and challenging. You would be a full member of the team."

"Right. Just like that."

"Yeah. Just like that. Don't stare at me as though this is something I should be ashamed of. I have connections, and I'm willing to use them to get what I want."

She glared at him. "Just when I start thinking how

great you are, you make me want to hit you with a large, blunt object."

She was really cute when she was mad. But he had a feeling telling her so wouldn't help his case. He gentled his tone. "You're right. It's only fair that I wait a few days before bullying you into taking a great job with a big paycheck in sunny Southern California."

A scoff escaped her. "Did you just say that you'll let it be for now? Because somehow I'm not feeling it."

He tried his best to look solemn and sincere. "I'm leaving it alone. For now."

She stood. "Thank you." And she turned for the door.

His heart sank to his boots. "Wait. Where are you going?"

"To my room."

"I just got you talking to me again, and now you want to leave?"

She paused with her hand on the doorknob. "I have some work I need to do. But I'll meet you downstairs at noon in the dining room. We can grab a couple of sandwiches and have a picnic in the park."

He'd been hoping at the very least to steal a kiss before he let her escape. *Have patience*, he told himself. But patience wasn't his strong suit—especially not where she was concerned. "A picnic sounds good."

"All right, then." And she pulled open the door and left him standing there alone by the window wishing it was noon already.

For lunch, Strickland's offered a variety of sandwich choices. The guests gathered in the dining room, where Melba served them beverages and took their orders.

As part of the family, Tessa went straight to the kitchen. She always made her own lunch, careful not to get in Claire's way. Today, she led Carson in there with her. Claire greeted them both and went back to work assembling a trio of club sandwiches.

"Roast beef? Turkey? Ham?" Tessa asked him.

Carson chose roast beef on rye. She made his sandwich and a turkey on whole wheat for herself. They grabbed two individual bags of chips, a couple of Claire's to-die-for chocolate chip cookies and a bottled water each, and headed for the park just down the street.

It was nice out, the day cool and bright. They found an empty picnic table under a big tree and sat down across from each other.

He'd no sooner unwrapped his food than he wanted her to share specifics about Della Storm, about what exactly had happened when Della fired her. He was pushing too hard again, and Tessa almost let her temper flare.

But then she caught herself. She took a moment to gaze at him across from her, heartbreaker handsome in a buff-colored jacket that hugged his broad shoulders over a white knit shirt that showed off his tan skin. And he was not only way too good-looking. He really did want to know about her, about her life, about what had made her the person she was.

How could she get mad at him?

She'd shut him down twice. Still, he'd knocked himself out to try to get close to her. He'd moved from the luxury and comfort of Maverick Manor to her grandmother's no-frills boardinghouse just for a chance to get to know her better.

If he wanted all the awful details of her past failures at life, work and love, well, so be it.

"I was no innocent victim, Carson. Don't even try to paint me as one. Yeah, Della was wildly jealous over Miles and vindictive about it. But I blew off a major project when I fell in love with him. It was as if my brain and ambition went on a long holiday, and all I wanted was to spend every moment with Miles. I'd never been in love before, never understood what other people thought was so important about finding 'the one.'" She dropped her sandwich to air-quote that for him. "And then I met Miles and—boom! I got it. I had no balance, you know? I went from being all about my career to being all about Miles, with no middle ground. I really messed up, and I fully deserved to suffer serious professional consequences."

He sipped from his water bottle. "You're too hard on yourself."

She loved that he defended her. But she couldn't agree. "You're entitled to your opinion. Even when you're wrong."

"So you're telling me you think you should be punished forever because of one mistake?"

"Well, Carson, it really was a doozy of a mistake. And I made it in a competitive field where second chances don't come easily."

"Just answer the question."

"Bossy much?" She opened her chips. "No, I don't think I should be punished forever. But I get why the big ad and design firms are going to be reluctant to hire me."

"Can you say with certainty that you would never screw up like that again?"

She felt pressured again and had to hold back a flippant response. It really was a good question, so she gave him a carefully considered reply. "I can say that I have definitely learned my lesson. I'll never leave colleagues or clients high and dry again. Life sometimes gets in the way of business, but if for some reason I couldn't hold up my end of a project, I'd be damn sure to keep communication open and find a way that the job would get done without me." She popped a chip in her mouth.

"All right. I have one more question."

"Of course you do." She waved another chip dramatically. "Go ahead. Hit me with it."

"Come to dinner with me in Kalispell tonight? Ryan told me about this great little Italian place."

She went with him.

How could she not? He charmed her and he challenged her. Every hour she spent with him, she found herself liking him more. And hey, the man was really easy on the eyes.

He ordered a nice bottle of Chianti and they shared an antipasto. She had ravioli. She also had a great time. He told her about his parents, who divorced when he was in his teens. His mother had remarried. Andrea VanAllen Drake Rivas had no other children. She now lived in Argentina with her second husband. His dad had died of a heart attack five years before.

She wanted to know more. "What about grandparents, aunts and uncles, cousins?"

"No grandparents living. I'm the only son of an only son. My mother has a sister, I think."

"You *think*?"

"They were never close, and I never met my aunt."

"I can't imagine being the only one. I have two sisters and grandparents on both sides. I have three uncles on my dad's side, aunts on my mother's side and a whole bunch of cousins. A Strickland family reunion is a thing of beauty, let me tell you. How long have you been running Drake Distilleries?"

"I took over when my father died. But I opened my first club two years before that. I wanted my own company, something I'd created from the ground up. Drake Hospitality has always been all mine."

"Clearly, there's nothing wrong with your work ethic, Carson."

"I like working, making things happen. My father encouraged me to get out there and see what I could do. He bankrolled my first club without even stopping to think it over. He used to talk about how rich kids often grew up lazy, lacking ambition. He said that I'd never had that problem and he was glad."

She could hear real affection in his voice. "You loved your father."

"Yeah. He was tough. Always one step ahead of the competition. And fearless. He loved the great outdoors, all the macho stuff—hunting and mountain climbing, sailing and stock-car racing. When he went after something, he got it. He taught me to shoot, took me hunting all over the world. I can't say I enjoyed it as much as he did, but if the day ever comes when I need to use a rifle to bring down some dinner, I'll be able to hit what I'm aiming at and take proper care of my weapon, as well. Maybe my dad was a little *too* driven. I think he lost my mother because he didn't have much time for her. And his doctors had been telling him to slow down for at least a decade before he had the heart attack that killed him."

"Would you say that you're like him?"

"In a lot of ways, yes. And proud to be. But I'm better at delegating, better at letting at least some things go." He gave her a smile that did something crazy to her heart. "So, tiramisu? Cannoli?"

"No, thanks. I couldn't eat another bite."

He waved her refusal away and ordered one of each. She ate some of each, too. More than a little. The desserts were too tempting to ignore.

Kind of like the guy across from her.

When they left the restaurant, the sun was half an orange ball sliding slowly behind the tall mountains. They got in his Cadillac, and she automatically went to latch her seat belt.

Carson's big, hot hand settled over hers. She glanced up sharply into those gleaming dark eyes.

One side of his sinful mouth kicked up. "Don't look so suspicious."

But she *was* suspicious. That very morning they'd agreed on friendship first. Not even twelve hours later, she knew from that look in his eye that he was about to kiss her.

Worse, she was about to let him.

Chapter Seven

"Carson," she said sternly—or at least she meant to sound stern. Actually, it came out on a soft hitch of breath.

"I can't stop myself," he whispered.

"Yes, you c—"

His lips took the word away before she finished saying it.

And an unfinished word wasn't all he took. He also laid claim to her will to resist him. He lifted his hand from hers and placed those long, strong fingers gently, carefully, along the side of her face, holding her. Capturing her with a caress.

Sweet heaven, the man could kiss. His mouth brushed across hers, teasing, coaxing, enticing her to let him take the kiss deeper.

She longed only to surrender to the feel of him, the heat of him.

With a small, hungry cry, she did what he wanted, opening to him, letting him in.

She would pay for this, and she knew that. She was giving ground too quickly. And for a man like Carson, that would only mean one thing: she would give some more.

It was all so simple, really. Awakened by the taste of him, her body, her heart, her foolish mind—they would all conspire to betray her for another kiss.

And another.

Easy. She was so easy. Half a day into this new "friendship" of theirs and she was kissing him like a whole lot more than just a friend. She should have more integrity, should stick by her plan to take things nice and slow.

But he'd blown right on by all her carefully erected boundaries. And it felt fabulous: the scent of him, the warmth of him so close, the flavor of him on her tongue. He tasted of coffee and chocolate, whipped cream and wonder, all wet and warm.

He was getting to her, stirring buried memories of Monday night. Sweet, sexy memories that hovered and swooped, taunting her, tempting her, just out of reach as his naughty tongue slid past her teeth and teased the wet places within.

A breathy moan escaped her as she gave to him further, letting her head drop back against the headrest. He didn't miss a beat, kept his mouth fused to hers. He leaned across the console, his fingers moving across her cheek, to her temple. He stroked her hair, soothing her, petting her. He traced the outer shell of her ear, caught her earlobe and rubbed it between his thumb and forefinger.

She moaned a little louder, and he shamelessly drank that sound from her parted lips.

Oh, she really shouldn't put her hands on him and she knew that.

But she did it anyway, bringing her palms up between them, easing them under the lapels of his jacket to press them against the hard, hot wall of his chest, telling herself she only meant to push him away.

That didn't happen.

Those traitorous hands of hers slid upward, loving the muscled feel of him beneath his white shirt, moving over the powerful shape of his shoulders to wrap around the back of his neck, to thread up into his hair.

The kiss went on and on. She didn't ever want it to end.

At the same time, she kept promising herself that she was going to stop it, put her hands back on his chest and gently push him away. She was doing that any minute now.

Very, very soon.

But in the end, she couldn't even manage that tiny triumph.

Oh no. He had her pressed against the seat back, his mouth locked to hers. And she had her arms around his neck as passionate echoes of Monday night drifted just out of reach in her reeling mind.

Lord help her, she never wanted to let him go.

And then *he* pulled back.

Just like that.

He broke the press of their lips, causing her eyes to pop wide-open. She stared straight into his. They were darker than ever, those eyes, full of heat and the promise of delicious pleasure.

"I know." he said ruefully, his voice so low and hot it could set the Cadillac on fire. "It's too soon."

She tried to pull herself together and somehow managed to mutter darkly, "Damn right it is."

"I was supposed to be giving you space, learning how to be your friend."

"That *was* the agreement."

"Tessa, I couldn't stop myself." His eyes smoldered—but she saw the gleam of humor in them, too, didn't miss the way he tried to keep those amazing lips from turning up at the corners.

She pressed her palms to his chest then and pushed him back a few inches more. "You didn't *want* to stop yourself."

"Can you ever forgive me?"

She regarded him patiently. "Stop messing with me."

"Kiss me again and prove you forgive me." He tried to swoop in.

But she was ready for him that time, stiffening her arms, keeping him at bay. "Not a chance. Get back in your seat. Drive the car."

He retreated behind the wheel—and started in about what they should do next. "So, how about the nightlife in Kalispell, Montana? I've been meaning to check out Moose's Saloon or maybe Scotty's Bar and Steakhouse..."

She slanted him a glance. Even from the side, he looked much too pleased with himself. "I think I've had enough thrills for one night. Home to the boardinghouse, please."

He turned those dark-velvet eyes to her and asked hopefully, "Scoreboard Pub and Casino?"

"Keep it up and I *will* make you pay."

"I am so looking forward to that." His eyes burned into hers, causing her skin to heat and the blood to race a little faster through her veins.

And then, finally, just before she blew it completely and reached across the console to grab his jacket in her fists and yank him close for another kiss, he pushed the start button and the Caddy hummed to life.

Tessa got downstairs for breakfast at six the next day. She grabbed a bagel and coffee and ran back up to work, hoping to get a few hours in before Carson came knocking on her door.

At a quarter of eight, she heard him leave his room. She waited for his knock.

It didn't come. He went on down the hall, and she went back to work, thinking he'd be upstairs again in no time.

But as far as she knew, he never came back up. She worked in her room all that morning, getting the ads Emmet needed emailed to the clinic, tackling a few other projects, then placing the ads and notices online as soon as Emmet gave the go-ahead.

At noon when she went down for lunch, she paused at Carson's door and debated whether or not to knock. When she gave in and tapped her knuckles against the wood, he didn't answer.

"Carson?" she called.

Nothing. Apparently, he wasn't in there.

She went down to the kitchen.

Claire, her clever fingers flying as she assembled sandwiches and garnished plates, asked, "So. You and Carson Drake, huh?"

Tessa got herself a cranberry juice from the fridge. "Friends. We are friends."

"How long's he in town for?" It was an innocent enough question.

Tessa felt defensive, anyway. But she took care to answer pleasantly. "A couple of weeks, I think."

"Ah," replied Claire, lining up plates.

Tessa couldn't stop herself from adding with a definite trace of sarcasm, "We have a good time hanging out together—you know, like *friends* do?"

"Well, all righty then." Claire scooped a pair of crispy golden Reuben sandwiches from the two-sided grill, sliced them in half diagonally and plated them.

"Auntie Tess! Hi there!" Bekka, sitting in her booster seat at the table enjoying crackers, banana slices and bits of chicken breast for lunch, slapped a plump hand on the table for attention.

Tessa went to her and got a gooey kiss, after which she couldn't stop herself from asking Claire, "And speaking of Carson, did you, um, happen to see him this morning?"

Before Claire could answer, their grandmother bustled through the open doorway from the dining room and announced, "He came down and had breakfast at a little before eight and left the house soon after." Melba pinned another order to the board above Claire's work area.

Grandma, you've got to stop lurking in the hallway, Tessa thought but didn't say. *And did he happen to mention when he'd be back?* She somehow kept herself from asking. "Thanks, Grandma."

"You're welcome, dear." Melba's smile was downright angelic.

Tessa took a plate, plunked a hunk of cheese on it, grabbed a knife, a napkin, a box of Triscuits and an apple, and went back upstairs to answer some queries that had come in through her website.

She worked for two more hours, with thoughts of Carson lurking in the back of her mind the whole time like a bad habit, the kind you were trying to quit, the kind that refused to let you go. She longed to dart out to the hallway and tap on his door, just to check and see if he might have returned without her hearing him come in. But somehow she kept herself from surrendering to that temptation. The poor man had a right to a little time to himself. And she had plenty to do, anyway.

Except for how she was getting downright stir-crazy. She'd been in her room for most of the day. Maybe a walk—to the park or over to Crawford's General Store. Anything to get out into the fresh air.

She walked to Crawford's, where she chatted with Natalie, Nate Crawford's lively younger sister, who was working the register that day. Tessa bought a five-gallon jar of Crawford's giant dill pickles. Claire liked to use them at lunch. Guests loved them.

Tessa hauled the heavy jar of pickles back to the boardinghouse and helped unload the dishwasher. She wiped down counters and pitched in to get the dining room set up for dinner.

Then she went down to the basement, where piles of clean linens waited for someone to fold them.

She was reaching for the next one from a pile of clean towels, when Carson asked from behind her, "Miss me?"

At the sound of his beautiful, warm, deep voice, Tessa felt the sudden hot press of tears behind her eyes. They burned at the back of her throat. Tears, of all the crazy things. She clutched the still-warm towel to her chest, stared at the concrete wall a few feet away and admitted with a forthright honesty that made her stomach clench, "Yes." She said it quietly, without turning. "I did."

His warm hand touched her shoulder, a brushing touch. She bit the inside of her cheek and swallowed the silly tears down. "Tessa. Hey." When she still didn't turn, he clasped her arm and slowly guided her around. Not a single tear had fallen; she'd called them back before they could. But still, her eyes were misty. She had no doubt he saw. "Tessa…" He looked at her so tenderly.

Always and forever, she would remember this moment. Standing in her grandmother's basement, clutching a warm white towel, while Carson Drake looked at her as though she was the only other person in the world.

"I should be more careful than this," she said. "I should know better than this. I hardly know you—"

"Tessa," he whispered, and that was all.

Just her name. It was enough. It was everything. Because of the way he said it—with so much promise, with hope. As though he wanted to reassure her that everything would work out right for them, even though she felt way too much for him, too soon. Even though she'd been here before and it had gone so badly.

Gently, he took the towel from her and tossed it back on the pile behind her. Then he gathered her close.

She went into his arms with no more than a surrendering sigh, cuddling against him much too eagerly, even going so far as to rest her cheek against the hard wall of his chest.

He kissed the crown of her head and explained, "My virtual meeting software doesn't get along very well with your grandmother's Wi-Fi."

She tipped her head back to look up at him. "I know. It's spotty. I wait forever for things to load."

He kissed her nose, right on the tip. She not only let him; she loved it. They shared one of those smiles, the kind that made her feel like they had about a hundred special secrets known only to the two of them. "I still have my suite at the Manor, so I went over there to get some work done."

"You need a room here *and* your suite at the Manor?"

"I thought I might need it for work. And I do. Plus, when I took the room next to yours, I wasn't sure how you'd react."

"Needed somewhere to run if I chased you out of here?"

"Exactly."

She thought that over and shrugged. "Hey. Makes perfect sense to me."

"You can join me there anytime, use the Wi-Fi, get your work done faster."

"Thanks. So far I'm managing, but I'll definitely keep your offer in mind."

"I grabbed a sandwich at the Manor Bar, where I ran into Mayor Traub, who invited me up to his house on Falls Mountain for dinner tomorrow. He promised to give me a tour of his saddle-making workshop. Did you know the guy makes these amazing custom saddles?"

"I did."

"The mayor also promised barbecued ribs—some special family recipe, he said. He told me that one of his cousins is *the* DJ Traub of DJ's Rib Shack fame."

Tessa had met *the* DJ Traub several times. "I know DJ. He lives down in Thunder Canyon now, with his wife and children. And did *you* know that Mayor Traub used to be plain old Collin Traub, who was about the baddest bad boy Rust Creek Falls has ever seen? No one could believe it when he and Willa Christensen fell in love. They'd been at odds practically since they were in diapers. Oh, and Collin and Nate Crawford grew up sworn enemies, too."

"Not possible. Those two are thick as thieves now, always plotting new ways to bring more business opportunities to this burg."

"Burg?" She shoved at his chest for that. "You'd better not let Collin or Nate hear you call our town a burg. They'll truss you up on Main Street in front of the town hall and let everyone throw rotten fruit at you."

He put up both hands and pretended to be terrified. "Don't let them hurt me."

"I won't be able to stop them. You need to remember to show some respect."

"I will, absolutely." He tried to look regretful. But he mostly just looked handsome and far too appealing for her peace of mind. "Collin said I should bring a friend tomorrow night. That would be you. Will you come?"

"Thank you, I will." She turned back to the table and picked up that towel again.

"Tessa..." He moved in closer and nuzzled her hair.

It felt simply glorious, just to have him near—and if she didn't keep her wits about her, she'd end up on her back with him on top of her faster than she could say the word *moonshine*. She faced him and put on her tough-girl voice. "Watch yourself there, friend."

"Tessa..." He said her name in a teasing whisper that time and tried to pull her close again. She snapped him with the towel. "Ow!"

"Go on upstairs. I'll be there in a few minutes. I just need to finish folding these."

He failed to obey, which didn't surprise her. Instead, he picked up a towel and folded it. No way had she expected that.

"Just being helpful," he said in response to her surprised glance.

They folded in silence, side by side, and she reminded herself not to get all dewy-eyed because the big-shot CEO was giving her a hand with the laundry.

That night, they stayed in and ate in the dining room. Later, they hung around in the downstairs sitting room with her grandparents. Carson seemed comfortable. He even agreed to play hearts when her grandfather pulled out a dog-eared deck and started shuffling. Tessa hauled the card table out of the hall closet, and Carson set it up for them.

Her grandma had a thousand and one questions for Tessa's new friend and she wasn't shy about asking them. Melba not only just *had* to know about his parents' divorce and his mother's remarriage, his father's death and the names of his nightclubs and restaurants, she also wanted to know if he'd ever been married.

Tessa tried to intervene at that point. "Grandma. Give the poor guy a break."

But Carson stepped right up. "It's okay, Tessa." He told her grandma, "I married my high school sweetheart the summer after our junior year at UCLA."

"But you got a divorce." Melba pursed her lips disapprovingly, as though just saying the D word left a bad taste in her mouth.

Carson explained how Marianne had wanted a family right away. "But I didn't. We keep in touch, though. And she's happy now, with the way it all turned out."

"I don't believe in divorce," declared Melba, as though that was going to be news to anyone. "But it appears you've had the best possible outcome of a failed marriage."

Tessa stifled a groan of embarrassment, but again, Carson didn't seem bothered in the least. He said, "My ex is a happy woman, and my life is good. It could have been a whole lot worse."

Her grandfather grunted. "Melba, your turn."

By the time Melba decided which card to play, the subject of Carson's ex-wife had been left behind.

Later, they sat out on the front porch, just Tessa and Carson, and talked until well past midnight. Then they walked up the stairs hand in hand. The whole way up, she thought about how much she wanted to kiss him.

But it was only the second day of their new "friendship," after all. She needed to keep the brakes on or she'd end up zipping right through the friend zone, headed straight for a full-blown affair.

Maybe she wanted that. Maybe they *would* end up in bed together again.

But not tonight.

When they reached her door, she wished him goodnight and ducked quickly into her room.

The next evening, they drove up Falls Mountain, past the spectacular wall of falling water that gave the mountain its name, to Collin and Willa Traub's beautiful, rustic house. Collin had inherited the house from a bachelor uncle and enlarged it, taking out walls, adding rooms and lots of windows. One wall of windows gave a spectacular view of the pine- and fir-covered mountains and of Rust Creek Falls, looking so small and quaint and charming in the valley below.

Collin led Carson down to his saddle-making workshop in the basement. Tessa stayed upstairs with Willa, a kindergarten teacher at RCF Elementary, and their baby boy who'd been born at the end of March. His name was Robert Wayne.

Willa insisted that Tessa hold him.

"Really, I'm just bad with babies," she tried to protest.

"No one is 'just bad with babies,'" Willa said. "Here."

Tessa gave in and took the baby. The second she curved her arms around him, little Robbie started wailing. "See? I warned you." Tessa handed the red-faced bundle back to his mom. "Babies hate me."

Willa smiled knowingly as she gathered Robbie close. "Wait till it's your own."

Oh, I plan to. Indefinitely. "I'm sure you're right,"

Tessa agreed. Because seriously, why argue? Babies were adorable and she totally loved them—they just didn't love her.

Willa cooed at her baby, and he settled right down. Tessa set the table as Robbie nursed. Then Willa took him to his room to change him and put him down.

"Out like a light," Willa said when she returned to the kitchen. "He's a good baby. If we're lucky, we'll get through dinner."

As they put the food on the table, Tessa explained how she was on the lookout for graphic design projects. "I'll take any job, no matter how small. I design everything from websites to yard sale ads to community car wash flyers. I'm hoping to get enough business going that I can move to Rust Creek Falls."

Willa suggested she check in at the high school. Maybe Tessa could teach a summer workshop in graphic design to boost her profile in the community. "And Kalispell isn't far. I'm sure you could find work there."

At dinner, the talk was mostly of plans Collin had to bring jobs and services to Rust Creek Falls. "Gotta tell you, Carson," he said. "I'm disappointed that you changed your mind about buying Homer's moonshine for Drake Distilleries."

Carson shook his head. "Sorry. Drake Distilleries is getting nowhere near that stuff."

Collin served himself another helping of ribs. "I was kind of hoping that the publicity might bring us more investors for our various projects around town."

"Trust me," Carson said. "Nobody needs *that* kind of publicity."

Tessa stuck a rib bone in the air. "Allow me to second that."

Willa and Collin shared a long look. Then Willa asked, "So, you guys tried it?"

Tessa glanced across at Carson. A little thrill shivered through her and she realized that somehow, in the past few days, the awful thing that had happened to them Monday night didn't seem so bad anymore.

Oh, she would never stop wanting to kick Homer's butt for being such an irresponsible, crazy old fool. But still.

The past couple of days had done a lot to change her mind about the whole thing. Now, no matter what happened between the two of them in the end, even if he flew back to LA tomorrow and she never saw him again, she would remember with fondness the night of the moonshine and how hard he'd worked afterward to get another chance with her. She would be glad that she'd known him. And that included her hazy recollections of what had happened in his bed.

"Okay, you two," Collin chided indulgently. "Your ribs will get cold."

Tessa realized she'd been sitting absolutely still, holding that same chewed-clean rib bone, staring into Carson's eyes for way longer than necessary. "Ahem." She set down the bone and blotted her lips with her napkin.

Willa prompted, "So, did you try the moonshine or not?"

Carson glanced Tessa's way again. At her quick nod of permission, he answered, "We did."

"And?"

"I'll say this. I don't think either of us will ever forget the experience—even though that stuff basically knocked us out cold."

Willa was nodding. "We had some, too. We drank the punch at the wedding picnic last Fourth of July."

She turned to look at her husband again, and her cheeks flushed pink.

Collin stared right back at her. "It tasted good. Really good."

Tessa asked, "Did it knock you out?"

"No, it didn't." Collin's voice had turned a little gruff, and his gaze was still locked on his wife. "I remember everything about that night. We went home early."

And then Willa chuckled. "Best Fourth of July ever."

Tessa just had to ask. "Robbie?"

Collin's bad-boy grin was slow and full of satisfaction. "Yep. Our little man's a Bonanza baby and that is no lie."

The next day, Sunday, Carson's cell rang at seven in the morning. He fumbled for the phone on the nightstand, peeled his eyes open and looked at the display. "What now, Ryan?"

"Kristen heard that you moved to Strickland's."

Carson yawned and shifted to get more comfortable in the slightly lumpy bed. "You said that Melba Strickland was the key. I went with that, more or less."

"Bold move. Clever."

"I try."

"Making progress with Tessa?"

"Last night I took her to dinner up at Collin and Willa's. It was great." She'd kissed him at her door when they said good-night, going on tiptoe, her soft hands sliding up and hooking around his neck, her high, firm little breasts pressing into his chest, her pliant mouth tasting of coffee and Willa's apple cobbler and the promise of more.

Ryan interrupted the sweet memory with a suggestion. "Feel free to thank me with a little Drake Imperial." The fifty-year-old special-edition Scotch sold for thirteen K a bottle.

"Your advice does not come cheap, my friend."

"Good advice never does. So what are you doing today? Kristen and I have an invite to her parents' place." The Daltons owned a ranch not far from town. "Bring Tessa. Dress for riding. We'll go up into the mountains and be back down in time for dinner with the folks."

Carson tapped on Tessa's door ten minutes later. She answered in a short satin robe, her hair loose on her shoulders, eyes a little droopy, lazy from sleep. It was a great look for her. She made his empty arms ache to hold her.

But he restrained himself.

"Ryan just called. He invited us to spend the day out at the Dalton Ranch. There will be horseback riding and then dinner with Kristen's family later."

She had her door partway open, leaning out to him, her slim body braced between the door and the frame. "Sounds like fun. I would love to go."

"Excellent. But you're crinkling your forehead. Is there a problem?"

"Well, I was just wondering if you've ever been on a horse."

It was so nice to feel smug. "I own a horse ranch. It's not far from Santa Barbara. I don't get out there as much as I'd like to. But it's a beautiful property. We raise and train Morgans and Thoroughbreds, mostly."

"So besides owning a *ranch* in *Santa Barbara*—" she drew out the emphasized words in a snooty tone "—you're saying you know how to ride a horse?"

"Yeah."

She wrinkled that beautiful nose at him. "Is there anything you don't know how to do?"

"Let me think it over. I'm sure there must be something."

"Humph. Dibs on the bathroom first."

"Wait a minute. Didn't you have it first yesterday morning?"

"Of course. I'm the *girl*. Girls get the bathroom first. They also take their time while they're in there. Deal with it." She tried to shut the door on him.

But he stuck his boot in it. "This is not a fair rule."

"Fair schmair. Sometimes life is just that way. Now get your foot out of my door so I can grab my caddy and have my shower."

He gave in and went downstairs to get a coffee while he waited for the use of the bathroom. It was ridiculously inconvenient.

And he couldn't remember ever having so much fun.

Tessa thoroughly enjoyed that day.

They spent most of it on horseback with Ryan and Kristen, riding up into the mountains, stopping often to enjoy the great views of the valley down below. When they got back down to the ranch late in the late afternoon, Kristen's mother had cold drinks waiting.

They all pitched in to set the table. Dinner was beer can chicken—you propped up the seasoned birds in a covered grill with a half-full can of beer in the cavity. The meat came out tender, juicy and full of flavor. Later, they all sat out on the Daltons' long front porch as the sun disappeared behind the mountains.

Tessa dropped off to sleep on the way back to town. When they got to the boardinghouse, Carson woke her with a kiss. Inside, they stopped to chat for a little with her grandparents and a few guests who were gathered in the sitting room.

Upstairs, Tessa got the bathroom first. He didn't even
give her a hard time about it. Once her teeth were brushed
and her face freshly washed, she lay in her bed in the dark
and thought how she hadn't been this happy in years.

It was like they were roomies, but with a delicious,
special edge of shared excitement and attraction. She
wished it would never end.

Of course, she knew that it had to. She knew that she
would stay in Montana and he had a life and a couple of
companies to run in Southern California. They might
think they could keep their connection, might promise
each other they would stay together in their hearts, that
thirteen hundred miles between them was nothing.

But realistically, long-distance relationships were impossible to maintain.

The next week went by way too fast. Tessa cut back on
her efforts to scare up work and refused to feel bad about
it. She wanted more time with Carson, and she took it.

He wouldn't be in town all that long, after all. And she
decided to savor every minute she might have with him.

They hiked just about every day, taking his SUV to
the edge of the forest and then setting out on foot, carrying snacks and cold drinks in their backpacks, heading
up the trails into the big trees.

Carson had a real understanding of the wilderness—
things his father had drilled into him, he said. He could
distinguish deer tracks from elk, tell coyote tracks from
a dog's. Once, they found bear tracks preserved in dried
mud. They were left by a black bear, he said. Grizzly
prints would be larger, with longer claw marks, the toes
closer together. The bear was long gone, he told her. No
scat and no fresh bear sign. She teased him that if he ever

got tired of running Drake Distilleries, he could always hire out as a tracker or wilderness guide.

On Saturday, as that week drew to a close, they rented horses from a local stable and rode out east, into the valley. Sunday, they did the same, riding toward the southwest that time, finding a nice spot on Rust Creek not far from the Crawford family ranch, where they went for a swim.

The water was icy cold. Still they laughed and splashed and dunked each other. And then they spread a blanket on the creek bank in the sun, wrapped their arms around each other and cuddled and kissed for over an hour.

Finally, he whispered against her parted lips, "We need to stop."

In response, she did exactly what she knew she shouldn't. She pressed her body closer to his, feeling the fine, hard ridge of his arousal against her belly. She wished she could melt right into him, hold on tight and never let go. She nibbled on his lower lip. "I don't ever want to stop."

He kissed a hot path down the side of her throat, smoothing her still-wet hair out of his way as he went. She moaned as he sank his teeth into the crook of her shoulder. "Come to the Manor with me. Stay there with me tonight." He breathed the words against her skin.

Oh, she wanted to. She was more than ready to spend a whole night with him. And this time, there would be no magic moonshine to leave her wondering what had really happened. This time, she would remember every moment, every touch, every thrilling, hungry sigh.

She kissed him eagerly, sifting her fingers through the damp silk of his hair.

When he lifted away that time, he levered back on his knees and reached for the shirt he'd thrown there when they went swimming. She lay in the sun and watched the play of light and shadow against the beautiful musculature of his chest until he went and covered it all up with that shirt.

"Tonight?" he asked again.

"Let me think about it."

And she did think about it, all the rest of that day. She thought how much she wanted the whole night with him—and the night after that. And after that.

She also reminded herself that spending a string of hot, sexy nights with him would only make it harder in the end to let him go.

That evening, after dinner, after a nice, long walk together in Rust Creek Falls Park, she told him she wouldn't be going to the Manor with him that night.

He didn't argue, just took her arm when they reached the edge of the park and pulled her under the shelter of a big oak. She waited with way too much anticipation for him to kiss her.

But he didn't. Instead, for the first time in a full week, he brought up the subject of that interview he wanted her to agree to, an interview with one of the biggest advertising firms in LA.

"Let me call them and set it up," he coaxed. "What do you have to lose? I'll fly you down there so you can check them out."

She laughed. "That's a good one. I think the idea is that *they* check *me* out—and I can buy my own plane ticket, thank you."

"Get there however you want to. Just promise you'll come if I get you the interview. And all I'm saying is that it doesn't have to cost you a thing. Just a little of your time. And you can stay with me in Malibu."

Okay, now *that* was tempting. To visit him in Malibu, to be with him there, where he lived…

She might be constantly telling herself not to get too close to him, but who did she think she was kidding? The minute he left her to return to his own life, she was going to start missing him. It was going to be tough.

"Say yes—" He framed her face in his big, warm hands. "To the trip, to the interview, to staying with me." He dropped a kiss in the middle of her forehead. "It's not a lifetime commitment. You can just say no to the job if it's not going to work for you."

She searched those dark eyes of his and found only tenderness and hope that she might give it a chance— both the job *and* this thing they had together.

Why not? asked a brave little voice deep down inside her.

He'd been nothing but wonderful to her. She needed to quit making up reasons to push him away.

And as for the job, she should stop being so negative. She wanted another chance at the career she'd trained for, apprenticed for, worked her butt off for. If she really could get a great job in LA, why shouldn't she go for it? Why shouldn't she try again? It wouldn't kill her to put off her dream of living in Rust Creek Falls for a few more years.

She needed to buck up, stop throwing away a great opportunity. She needed to be braver. To stand tall and take a real chance or two in life again—and just maybe in love, as well.

"Tessa?" He was watching her, looking more than a little worried. "You're too quiet. What are you thinking?"

She went for it. "I'm thinking I need to thank you, Carson."

He looked more wary than flattered. "Thank me for what?"

"For pushing me to take a damn chance again."

His mouth twitched with the beginnings of a smile. "You're welcome."

"Go ahead and call your guy at IMI. Set up the interview. I'll come visit you in Malibu, and we'll see how it goes."

Chapter Eight

The next morning after breakfast, Carson went to Maverick Manor where the Wi-Fi was dependable. He had a virtual meeting scheduled for ten o'clock with the Drake Distilleries management team.

But before that, he called Jason Velasco at IMI. After the usual how're-you-doing chitchat, he told Jason about Tessa and said he'd seen her work, considered her brilliant and talented and wanted Jason to take a look at her for IMI.

He gave Jason her website address. "Tessa worked in New York for a couple of years, but then moved back to her hometown of Bozeman, Montana. And I have some examples of her work here with me," he added, meaning the sketchbook from the night of the moonshine. "She drew up a whole moonshine campaign for me on the fly."

"You mean the moonshine campaign that isn't going to happen?" Jason asked.

"That's the one. But I thought it might be useful to you. It'll give you another angle on how damn good she is. I'll get that to you overnight."

"How, exactly, do you see us proceeding with this?"

"Look over her stuff. Vet her. Then have her in for an interview and see where it goes from there."

"She's now in Bozeman, Montana, you said? What's the name of her firm there?"

"She works freelance. I'll have her fly down to you when you're ready to interview her." Carson really didn't want to get into the part about Della Storm firing her. What if Tessa had overestimated the problem? He didn't want to make her look bad if Jason didn't even need to know.

Then again, Jason would be hiring her to a large degree on Carson's say-so. The man had a right to know the basic story as Tessa had explained it.

So he told Jason a generalized version of what Tessa had told him, excluding any mention of that douche canoe, Miles Rutherford, instead citing "personal issues" as the reason Tessa had lost focus on her work and ended up being discharged.

Carson also left out the part about how the Storm woman had blackballed her. Legally, Della Storm could do nothing of the sort, and four years had passed since all that had gone down. Maybe Tessa's former boss was willing to let bygones be bygones by now.

When Carson finished the story, Jason said he'd heard of Della Storm, that she was a household name in the ad game. Then he asked, "And since Della Storm let her go, Tessa Strickland has only worked freelance, you said?"

"Look at it this way. Now you know she's a find. Della Storm wouldn't work with anyone second-rate."

"That's an interesting take on the situation." At least

Jason chuckled when he said it. "Okay, Carson. I'll do my homework on this, and we'll go from there."

"Can't ask for more."

"I'll get back to you if I have questions."

"Please do. I'll mail you these sketches."

"And I'll let you know when we're ready to move on to the next step."

"Meaning the interview," Carson clarified.

"Yes. Meaning the interview."

"Terrific. I appreciate this, Jason. And I can't wait to see what you and your team have for us next week."

Jason went on for a few minutes about how excited he was to show off the campaign for the flavored liqueur launch. Carson made the right noises in response and then, finally, they said goodbye.

After Carson took his virtual meeting, which lasted two hours, he packed up Tessa's sketchbook to send to Jason and added it to the stack of outgoing mail in the foyer of his suite. The Manor's concierge would take care of it from there.

By the time he finally got back to the boardinghouse, Melba told him that Tessa was down in the basement dealing with laundry. He ran down the backstairs, eager to see her.

She was bent at the waist, stuffing wet sheets in a dryer when he found her.

"Don't straighten up," he advised. "Things look great from here."

She called him a bad name under her breath and did exactly what he'd asked her not to do, rising to her full five-foot-three, shoving the door shut and starting the machine. The sheets inside began to tumble as she turned to face him. He grabbed her hand and pulled her close, wrapping his arms around her, burying his nose against her throat so he could breathe in the scent of her.

She sighed and let her hands slide up to hook around his neck. "Hello, Carson."

They shared a kiss. God, he loved the taste of her.

When he lifted his head, she asked, "Busy morning?"

He bent close again and rubbed his cheek against her hair. "I had a long online meeting." He sighed. "And I miss my assistant. I had to address several envelopes all by myself."

She faked a sympathetic look, not a very good one. "Oh, you poor thing. You must be exhausted."

"My fingers are worn to the bone." He held them out to her. "Kiss them." Wearing a very serious expression, she did just that, one by one. He watched those soft lips brush his fingertips and wished he could freeze time in that moment, with her standing so close, her gold-flecked eyes shining up into his. "Thank you," he said once she'd kissed all eight fingers and his thumbs, as well. "I feel so much better now."

"Good. Help me." She grabbed a sheet from the table by the machines. He helped her fold, taking one side, following her cues, until the large sheet was a tidy square. They started on the next one. "So…did you talk to your guy at IMI about me?"

He brought her up to speed on that situation. "I hope you're not pissed that I said you fell down on the job."

She gave him a glowing smile for that. "Are you kidding? A little honesty is never a bad thing."

"Good." Relief released the slight knot of tension between his shoulder blades. He *had* been worried she'd be upset that he'd said so much. "I left that Miles character completely out of it, just said you had 'personal issues,' so when it comes to the interview, you can take that in whatever direction you want. And I never said anything about your being blackballed, either."

She tipped her head sideways and gave him a thoughtful look. "You're sure there will even be an interview?"

"I am, absolutely."

A low, amused sound escaped her. "It must be wonderful being you. You just say jump, and all your minions ask how high."

He gave her a shrug. "Someone has to rule the world. I think I should get another kiss for being so helpful to your career."

She handed him one end of yet another sheet. "You're always finding some reason that you should get another kiss."

He reached out, wrapped an arm around her and hauled her close. "Give me my kiss."

She whipped her side of the sheet quickly around her other arm before it could hit the concrete floor. "Oh, fine. Take it."

So he did. A long one. Until she pushed against his chest and demanded, "Get folding." He stepped back, and the whole process began again.

As they came together and then stepped away, she said softly, "I feel kind of bad."

"Why?"

"I think I've made Miles seem worse than he was."

"Worse? How could that bastard be worse? He cheated on you, and he set you up so you walked in on him in the act. He rubbed your nose in it. The man gives new meaning to ugly."

"He, um, he did propose to me. Several times."

"So? He still cheated. You made the right choice to tell him no."

"All I'm saying is, maybe he got tired of waiting for me to say yes."

"So what? He didn't deserve a yes."

"But, Carson, at the end, after I caught him with the twins, when I was packing my bags to go, he told me that he'd given up on me because I kept turning him down."

"He actually said that?" At her sad little nod, he said exactly what he thought of Miles Rutherford's excuses. "If he was so damned upset that you wouldn't say yes, he should have told you so then, and tried to work it out with you. After that, if you still wouldn't meet him halfway, he should have broken it off. Relationships aren't rocket science, Tessa. A guy needs to stand up and behave with integrity. If he doesn't, he gets what he damn well deserves." He saw the gleam in her eyes and went on before she could start in on him. "And yeah, I've been with more women than I probably should have. I blew up my marriage to a wonderful wife. I wasn't ready to be married, and I damn well should have figured that out before I broke Marianne's heart. I'm not perfect. But I don't tell lies, and I don't cheat." He moved close and gave her his side of the mostly folded sheet.

She made the last few folds and set it on the stack. "You're right," she said at last. "I didn't really trust Miles, not deep in my heart. I felt so inexperienced. I *was* inexperienced. I didn't want to make some huge mistake, you know? And it turned out he wasn't worth trusting, anyway."

"Now you're seeing what really happened there."

"Which doesn't say a whole lot for my judgment, does it?"

He gave her a stern look. "Name me one person on earth who hasn't been guilty of bad judgment at one time or another."

She hummed low in her throat. "I do feel bad that I screwed Della over, though. She was tough as nails, but she was fair. I think she would have gotten over my relationship with Miles if I hadn't left her high and dry on that last project."

"So get a message to her. Apologize."

She gave him a wide-eyed look. "Seriously? Won't she just think I'm kissing up when IMI contacts her?"

"Tessa, it's what *you* think that matters."

Her smile bloomed then, a wide one. "You know, I just might do that."

"Good."

He backed her up against the folding table and claimed another kiss, after which they finished folding the rest of the sheets and went upstairs for lunch.

Once they'd eaten, she said she had work to do and shut herself in her room for a few hours. He let her go reluctantly.

They had six days left until he had to return to LA. Yeah, he had high hopes that she'd agree to take the job with IMI. He couldn't wait to show her how much she was going to love living in California.

But who knew how long it would take to get the job thing settled, to get her moved so she lived nearby? He could be weeks without her. Months, even.

So right now, while he had the chance, he wanted to spend every possible minute with her. Was he falling too damn fast and way too hard for her?

So what if he was?

The way he saw it, his strong feelings for her were all the more reason to steal every second he could with her.

That evening, he'd agreed to meet for drinks at the Manor bar with Walker Jones, the millionaire entrepreneur who was opening a new day care center in Rust

Creek Falls. Tessa went with him. Both Nate Crawford and Collin Traub were there, too. Nate had brought his wife, Callie, which worked out great. She and Tessa were already casual friends and happy for a chance to catch up.

Walker Jones's day care empire was called Just Us Kids, and the one in Rust Creek Falls would be opening the second week of July. Nate joked that Just Us Kids was "just in time." The only other day care in town, Country Kids, had a waiting list now, what with all the babies born that spring.

Walker was a good-looking, confident guy who seemed a little more interested in empire building than in the particulars of how the new Rust Creek Falls day care center would be run. But Carson was big into empire building himself, so he didn't fault Jones for having a lot of ambition. They exchanged contact info and promised to stay in touch.

Afterward, when everyone left, it was just Carson and Tessa. They ordered burgers right there in the bar.

Their food had just arrived when she said, "Thanks for the pep talk this afternoon."

He leaned close. The way he saw it, the closer he got to her, the better. Her hair shone in the glow from the lights above and he didn't think he'd ever seen eyelashes as thick and silky as hers. "It wasn't a pep talk. I just said what I believe."

She dredged a French fry in ketchup and popped it into her mouth. "Well, I appreciate it. And I took your advice about Della. I wrote her a letter—you know, on actual stationery. I don't know why exactly, but on nice paper, it all seemed more serious, more sincere somehow."

"I get that, yeah."

"I told her how much I respect her and how much I learned from her and also how much I regret blowing that last account. I apologized for that and wished her well. And then I mailed it before I could think of a thousand reasons not to."

"Well done." He stared at her for a solid count of five and thought that he would never grow tired of looking at her.

She leaned a little closer. "I really like you, Carson. I mean, I really, *really* like you."

He couldn't resist, so he didn't. He leaned closer still, brushed a kiss across her soft cheek and whispered in her ear, "I like you more."

She giggled. It was about the most beautiful sound he'd ever heard. And then she said, "Look. Down here." She dipped that dark head toward her lap, where she held her small purse wide-open between her hands. Inside, he saw a toothbrush and a bit of cream-colored satin.

His chest felt suddenly tight. So did his pants. He leaned in again and whispered, directly into her ear that time. "Panties? You brought panties?"

She backed away a fraction, enough that she could meet and hold his gaze. "A girl needs clean panties. And a toothbrush, too. At least she does if she's planning on staying the night."

Chapter Nine

Tessa stood in the doorway from the bathroom in Carson's suite. She wore only a black lace bra and panties to match. She'd never been so nervous in her life.

"Come here." Carson's voice was deep, a little bit rough—and very sure. He'd gotten undressed while she used the bathroom, and now he rose from the bedside chair and faced her in only a pair of dark boxer briefs.

Oh, my Lord. The man was so beautiful. How did he have time to keep a honed, cut body like that while running two corporations and chasing down crazy moonshine makers in the wilds of Montana?

He held out his hand to her.

A sound slipped from her—half sigh, half moan. She could not believe this was actually happening. It didn't feel quite real.

Oh, but it was. Her bare feet whispered across the polished wide-plank floor and then were silenced completely when she reached the thick pile of the bedroom rug. Three more steps and she stood before him.

"Tessa." Her name came out on a low husk of breath. And then he touched her. With one slow, deliberate finger, he traced a line from the hollow of her throat straight down to the little black bow between her small breasts. "I've waited forever for this." That finger went roaming, stirring a trail of heat and hunger in its wake, up the gentle curve of one breast, back down, and up over the other.

She somehow couldn't stop her mouth from arguing. "It hasn't been *that* long. We've only known each other— oh!" The breathless sound escaped her as he took her by the shoulders and pulled her tight against that big, hard body of his. It felt so good. That hardness. That heat.

He bent his head and rubbed his deliciously scruffy cheek against hers. "You are perfect."

"Well, no, I'm—"

"Don't argue." His hand strayed behind her.

"But…" She forgot whatever it was she meant to say as she felt the quick brush of his knuckles against the middle of her back right before her bra came undone. She barely had time to gasp in surprise before he had the straps sliding along her arms and was pulling it down from between them, whipping it up and tossing it over his shoulder.

"Perfect." He clasped her waist and then eased both hands upward along her rib cage to cover her breasts with his big palms. His thumbs dipped in to rub her nipples, making them ache, bringing a long, breathy moan from her. "I've never known anyone like you," he whispered. "I hardly know what to do with you. I only know that from the first minute I saw you, Tessa, in that stork suit on that silly float, holding Kayla's baby, looking adorable and miserable and too cute for words, I knew I *had* to meet you, to know you, to hold you like this."

She stared down at his hands. They felt so good engulfing her breasts. With a slow sigh, she lifted her gaze to meet his. "I was so scared that day when you saw me, when you stared at me and I stared back at you. I felt as though you and I were the only two people in the world, as though Main Street and the Baby Bonanza Parade and every single citizen of Rust Creek Falls had vanished. There was just us, and I was terrified."

"Terrified?" He frowned down at her, dark eyes velvet soft. "Why?"

"The attraction I felt for you was so strong, so… instantaneous. It really scared me. It was too much like what had happened with—"

He cut her off with a quick shake of his head.

She understood. She didn't want to say another man's name right now, anyway. Because there *was* no other man. Just this one. Just Carson. "I…didn't want to go there again."

He made a chiding sound. "This is nothing like what happened before. You're with me now. I've told you I won't cheat." He repeated, "This is nothing like before."

But how long will it last? And what if it ends badly? What if you break my poor heart?

The questions tumbled over themselves in her mind. And why wouldn't they? After all, she was doing exactly what she'd promised herself she wouldn't do, taking the kind of emotional risk she'd sworn never to take again. And, no, Carson really wasn't like Miles. Except for being too good-looking and having too much money— oh, and giving off an air of undeniable power and self-confidence.

And the women. Even if he'd promised not to cheat

and she actually believed him, he'd admitted openly that he'd been with a whole bunch of women.

He bent close, caught her earlobe between his white teeth and worried it gently, unleashing a flood of sensation inside her, hot little shivers that skittered down her nerve endings. "You're thinking too much. Stop."

And then he banded those big arms around her, hard. Her bare breasts pressed flat against his broad, hot chest. She could feel everything, every beautiful muscle, including the long, thick hardness between his muscular thighs.

"Oh!" she gasped again—her vocabulary reduced to one silly exclamation—as he grasped her bottom in both hands and lifted her. "Yes," she sighed, raising her legs, wrapping them around him nice and tight.

His mouth came down on hers. She opened to him instantly, kissing him with eager yearning as he carried her to the bed. His tongue skimmed the wet surfaces beyond her parted lips. She sucked on it shamelessly, rolled her own tongue around it. He tasted so good. She could kiss him forever.

She loved the way he touched her, so tenderly and yet with such hunger. He laid her down on the bed so carefully, as though she were infinitely precious to him. And then he took his mouth from hers and looked into her eyes. "I need to see you. All of you. I need you bare."

She couldn't agree fast enough. "Yes. Bare. Please. You first."

That took about a second. He lifted the waistband of his boxer briefs over the bulge of his erection, shoved them down his legs and kicked them off.

He was so fine. A smile trembled across her lips.

He smiled back, slowly, a naughty smile that promised a whole night full of sweet, hot delights. And then he took her panties by the elastic and guided them down.

She lifted her head from the pillow and watched as he slid them past her thighs, over her knees, all the way clear of her lavender-painted toes. He tossed them off the end of the bed.

"So damn pretty," he declared, gently easing her thighs apart, revealing her most secret, intimate flesh to his gaze. "Beautiful."

It had been so long since a man had looked at her this way, so possessively, with a hunger that promised he would devour her. Not for years. *No, wait.*

The night of the moonshine. Carson had looked at her that way then. But how could that count when she could only remember it in a vague and hazy way?

A horrible thought occurred to her. She gasped and bounced up onto her elbows.

He stopped tickling the back of her knee to ask, "What's the matter?"

"Condoms. I forgot to ask. I just assumed you would have them."

"Shh." His hand went roaming. He caressed his way up to the top of her thigh.

She gasped again, partly in response to his touch and partly because there was no way they were going any further without condoms, no way she was driving to Kalispell for the morning-after pill again. "But, Carson—"

"You assumed right. I have them. Now, lie back."

Relieved, she dropped her head onto the pillows again as his hand strayed higher. He traced a slow path inward and then up even higher, over the narrow strip of dark hair she'd left when she'd groomed herself so carefully to be ready for him tonight.

And then, at last, he parted her, touching her where she wanted him most. "Wet," he whispered approvingly. Followed by, "Finally, Tessa. Finally."

She might have said yes. She might have said anything as he parted her, stroking her, making her wetter still, dipping one finger in and then another. She moved with him, her body rocking in rhythm with his knowing touch. No way could she keep herself from lifting, opening her legs wider, offering him more.

When he lowered his mouth to her, she cried out.

He made soft, soothing sounds as he kissed her there, where she burned for him. Oh, it was so good. So fine. Just what she'd needed from him for so long now—for these past two weeks of too-brief days that also somehow felt like forever.

He guided her knee up, eased those wide shoulders under her thigh and settled between her parted legs. He kissed her some more, deeply, thrillingly, using his hands, too, to take her higher and higher, until she cried out as fulfillment found her. Clutching his dark head, holding him there, she lost herself completely, her climax drawing down to a pinpoint of heated light and then flaring, spreading out from the center of her like the spokes in a burning wheel.

He stayed with her, touching her, kissing her, drawing the pleasure out, so that it kept pulsing through her for the longest, sweetest time.

At the end, she wanted him closer, wanted to feel him all along her yearning body, skin to skin. She fumbled, grabbing for him, pulling on his shoulders, stroking his hair.

Finally he freed himself from the cage of her open thighs and slid up her body. He gathered her close to him, wrapping her up in those big, hard arms of his. She breathed in the scent of him, soap and that subtle aftershave he wore. And man.

All man.

It was wonderful. Exactly right. She laid her head against his chest and listened to the strong, steady beat of his heart as he cradled her close.

And then she was ready all over again, yearning for more.

Because really, who knew how long this thing with them would last? Who could say?

She only knew she was in it now, her hungry heart open, wanting. Needing. Hoping for more.

Better not to waste a moment.

She ran her seeking fingers downward, over the hard curves of his chest, along the rocklike ripples of those beautiful abs until she found him and wrapped her hand around him.

She stroked him, learning the beautiful shape of him.

"Harder," he commanded in a low growl.

She was only too eager to comply, squeezing him tighter, sliding her hand roughly up and down the shaft, rubbing her thumb over the sleek flare, spreading the moisture that wept at the tip.

He kissed her as she stroked him, kissed her hard and deep and wild.

And then, with a feral groan, he reached between them and stilled her hand. She tried to override him, to keep stroking, keep pleasuring him.

But he wouldn't have it. "Not like this." He kissed the words onto her parted lips. "Together."

Still, she held on. It felt so good to claim him that way, to have the power to make him wild.

"Behave." He growled the word. He pressed his forehead to her forehead. And then, a little raggedly, "Please."

Reluctantly, she released him. He reached across her to the nightstand on her side, slid open the drawer and took out a condom. She watched as he tore off the top foil strip with his teeth, got it free of the packet with a quick twist of his long fingers.

He rolled it down over himself.

And then he was reaching for her again, turning her to her side, facing him. His mouth took hers as his warm hand slid down over the curve of her back, one long stroke over her hip to her thigh. He lifted her leg, guiding it over to wrap around him, positioning her for him so that he slid into her waiting heat in one smooth, thrilling glide.

They kissed endlessly, their mouths fused as though sealed together, never, ever to let go. And then he started to move, withdrawing so slowly, then returning, only to withdraw once more. Each time he retreated, she almost lost him.

More than once, he chuckled against her mouth, cruel and tender, as she begged him with her lips and her body, with her arms around him and her leg wrapping him hard and tight, holding him to her.

Please, please don't go.

Never go.

Stay.

He picked up the rhythm, pulsing faster against her, going deeper, retreating farther, though surely that wasn't possible. Each time, she knew she would lose him. Until he came back to her, filling her so perfectly, going deeper still. She felt him all through her, into the heart of her. He claimed her, all of her, thrilling her, carrying her away to a place where there was only pleasure. Only him. His big body taking her, his eyes searing into hers, his touch burning her in the most shocking, delicious way.

Like a wave, he rolled over her, rising, crashing into her, filling her so full with him, so that all she wanted was the feel of him, the touch of his mouth on her skin, the warmth of his breath in her ear.

Carson, I love you.

Dear, sweet Lord in heaven, she'd almost said it. How totally foolish would that have been? She'd known him for exactly two weeks as of that very night. Nowhere near enough time to start talking about love.

But some shred of sanity remained to her. She kissed him harder and kept those words in.

And he kept on moving, pushing so deep within her, driving her higher, until she was lost again, the coil of heat and wonder opening wide within her. She let out a cry as her climax rolled through her.

He guided her onto her back then. She lifted her legs and twined them around him. He levered up on those muscled arms and moved harder and faster, went deeper than ever.

Dazed, dreamy, her own finish still rocking her in thrilling aftershocks, she saw the shudder of greater pleasure sweep through him, felt him pulsing within her as his climax took him down.

They made love again an hour later. Tessa thought it was even more beautiful than the first time.

More tender, less desperate, the hungry edge not quite so sharp. He filled her body and her heart.

Love. Dear Lord, I love him.

She wasn't supposed to do that, had thought she'd learned her lesson, had promised herself never again to fall so hard and so fast.

Later, she decided. She would think about it later. He was leaving in five days. She would enjoy every second she had with him till then.

And after that, well, they would see, wouldn't they?

Maybe there would be a job offer from IMI, as he kept insisting was guaranteed to happen. By then, she would have a better idea of what to do.

Or at least, she hoped she would.

"Tessa." He nuzzled her neck, wrapped her hair around his fist. "God. I can't get enough of you. The scent of you, the feel of your skin, those soft little sounds you make when I touch you, all of it, all you do. You drive me wild."

And then he was kissing her, touching her all over, turning her onto her stomach, doing very naughty things to her...

Twenty minutes later, he left her just long enough to get rid of the condom. When he returned to her in the tangled bed, he wrapped her close, pulling her back against him, spoon-style. "Sleep now."

"Umm..." She was already drifting off.

Long after midnight, he woke her again with slow, drugging kisses. She moaned and told him to go back to sleep.

At first.

But he only kept kissing her, kept touching her, arousing her. Soon enough, she was every bit as eager as he to make love yet again.

They didn't get to sleep again until almost four.

Sometime later, she woke to the smell of coffee. He was bending over her, wearing unbuttoned jeans and a tempting smile. "Eggs and bacon?"

"Perfect."

He served her breakfast in bed, after which they greeted the morning with more lovemaking, her slight soreness from the night before quickly turning to excitement and pleasure.

After that, she took a long, slow bath in the suite's

huge jetted tub as he made a few calls to LA and caught up on his messages.

They returned to the boardinghouse for lunch, taking sandwiches to the park the way they liked to do. Later, after she'd put in a couple of hours helping her grandmother and Claire, they hiked into the mountains, where they spread a blanket in the sun and made love beneath the wide Montana sky.

That night they returned to the Manor and went to bed early, though not to sleep.

After that, the days settled into a glorious rhythm. Mornings were for working. And the afternoons, evenings and late into the night were for the two of them. The hours flew by. She wished she could grab each moment and hold it close, so that this precious time they shared would never end.

On Thursday afternoon, Carson told Tessa that IMI would be calling her. On Friday, she got that call. She agreed to an interview at their Century City offices on the following Thursday.

Too soon, it was Saturday. Carson would leave for Los Angeles on Sunday.

That night they had dinner at the Manor bar and then went up to his suite, where they fell on the bed together, kissing desperately, popping more than a few buttons in their eagerness to eliminate the flimsy barrier of their clothing. They made love as though they would never see each other again.

And then, as they lay together afterward, holding each other close, he tipped up her chin, stared hard into her eyes and said, "Come with me tomorrow. Move in with me in Malibu. You can work from there as well as here. And there will be a great job for you with IMI, anyway."

She opened her mouth to speak.

But he shook his head and went right on. "I want you with me. I know it's fast, but I don't give a damn. I haven't felt like this since…oh, who am I kidding? I've *never* felt like this. I don't want to walk away from it. I want us together."

Yes! cried her hungry heart. But she needed to be smarter than that. She needed not to make the same mistakes she'd made with Miles. "Carson, I—"

His eyes flashed with angry heat. "No. Don't start with the excuses. Don't compare me to that cheating loser who didn't have sense enough to take care of what mattered, who was too much of an idiot to treat you right."

"I'm not comparing you to him."

"The hell you're not."

"I'm not. I just can't go with you now."

"You *can.*"

"I can't. Not right now. I really can't just throw over all my plans so suddenly. I need to do this my way. I'll come down for the interview with IMI, I promise. That's less than a week from now. I'll stay a day or two with you then. But we have to slow down a little. Please try and understand."

He dragged her close and kissed her, a hot, angry, punishing kiss, a kiss she reveled in—until he ended it by grabbing her arms again and pushing her away. "No," he said much too softly. "I don't understand." And then he shoved back the covers and left her.

Clutching the sheet against her chest, she watched him stride naked to the bathroom. He shut the door behind him harder than he needed to.

Tessa waited, feeling miserable, having to hold herself in place there in the bed, to keep herself from tiptoeing to the bathroom door, from tapping on it gingerly, from promising to do whatever he wanted if only he would let her in.

He came out on his own a few minutes later and rejoined her in the bed.

And then he apologized. "I was out of line. I'm sorry. I just… I don't want to leave you, but my businesses aren't going to run themselves."

She kissed him and stroked the hair at his temples, pressed her palm against his scruff-rough cheek. "I hate that you're going. I only want to be with you, but I need to take this slower. Please."

Reluctantly, he agreed to do it her way.

In the morning, he checked out of Maverick Manor and they returned to the boardinghouse. He packed up his things there.

They'd already agreed that he would drive himself to Kalispell where his plane waited. He said goodbye to her grandparents and her sister.

She followed him out to the Cadillac. He kissed her one last time right there in the parking lot, a long, slow one that she wished might never end.

Much too soon, he was pulling away and getting behind the wheel. "I'm sending a plane for you next Wednesday. You can stay with me Wednesday night, be fresh for the interview Thursday. Don't argue with me about it."

She gave him a trembling smile. "Thank you." And then she stood in the bright late-morning sunshine and watched him drive off, her heart aching as though she'd just ripped it in two.

Chapter Ten

The next few days were awful. Tessa missed him terribly. Her whole body seemed to ache with longing for him—which, really, was ridiculous. She would be seeing him again in three days, on Wednesday, when he flew her to him in LA.

And he kept in close touch, carrying on a constant conversation with her via text. Plus, two or three times a day, one or the other of them would find a reason they just *had* to talk to the other immediately. Then they would play phone tag until whoever couldn't talk was available—often that would be at night, when his long workday was through. Those calls inevitably ended in really good phone sex.

She truly was never out of contact with him. But she yearned for him, anyway. And every minute she wasn't on the phone with him dragged by in slow motion.

There was another slight problem, too. As of Monday, her period was officially late.

But she refused to worry over it, reminding herself that it had been late before and always came eventually. And hello! Three condom wrappers *plus* the morning-after pill. How could she possibly be pregnant? It made no sense.

It was the excitement, that was all, of being wildly in love, of longing for Carson. Not to mention the upheaval of not really knowing what to do about it all.

Should she follow her heart to LA, change her life for him—as she'd done for Miles? Or should she stick with one of her earlier plans, which weren't all that solid, either: stay in Bozeman, or try to make a go of it in Rust Creek Falls?

Finally, Wednesday morning came. At nine fifteen, she boarded Carson's plane at the Kalispell airport. When the plane touched down in Santa Monica, he had a car waiting for her. Forty-five minutes later, she was greeted at his front door by his housekeeper, Sharon, who took her suitcase to the master suite and gave her a quick tour of Carson's gorgeous, modern house, one whole side of which—the one facing the Pacific—was made of glass.

There was a gym in the basement and an infinity pool beyond the wall of windows—a whole section of which rolled up like a big garage door, making it possible to combine the living room and the massive deck into one beautiful indoor-outdoor room. The kitchen was enormous, all stainless steel and stark white cabinetry, with top-of-the-line appliances.

Sharon explained that dinner was ready to be popped into the oven and an assortment of cheeses and meats, fresh fruits and crudités, along with fresh-baked bread and several varieties of crackers, were all ready and waiting for her should she feel like a snack.

If none of those suited, the pantry was full and there

was more to choose from in the fridge. Sharon jotted her number on the pad at the end of the counter. "Just in case you need anything that I might be able to help you with. The beach is lovely today," she added. "Simply take the stairs down at the edge of the deck. Should you need a suit, check the cabinets in the cabana."

Then, with a warm smile, Sharon left. She was barely out the door when Tessa's cell rang.

It was Carson. "How was your flight?"

"Smooth." She pressed a finger to the side of her throat, where her pulse had quickened at the sound of his voice. "The limo driver was there waiting for me when I arrived. I feel thoroughly spoiled. And Sharon is a treasure."

"I need to see you." His voice had gone darker. It burned in her ear.

Heat flooded her, a lovely heaviness down low made up of longing and delicious anticipation. "Come home, then. I'm right here."

He arrived an hour later, swept her into his arms and took her to bed, where they remained for three hours. Then he had to go back to the office for a late meeting. She found a bikini in the cabana and went down to the water for a long stroll along the beach.

Carson returned a little after seven. They ate the dinner Sharon had prepared for them, and he opened a bottle of very expensive champagne he'd bought to celebrate their reunion.

She thought of her period that hadn't come yet and took a pass on the bubbly.

"You okay?" he asked, watching her much too closely.

"I'm fine. I…"

"What?"

No. Uh-uh. She was not discussing her menstrual

cycle now. She rallied with, "Remember how I told you after the night of the moonshine that I would never drink again?"

He gave her his most patient look. "Tessa, this is a 1996 Krug Clos d'Ambonnay."

She took his glass from him and had a sip. "Delicious. Spectacular." She handed it back. "I'm honored you would open it for me. And that's all I'm having."

He shrugged then and teased, "More for me," and let it go at that, for which she was grateful.

They went to bed early, ostensibly so that she could get her beauty sleep. That didn't happen.

Not that she cared. His touch not only set her on fire; it pushed back all her worries—about where to go from here, about the real reason she'd turned down his expensive champagne.

In the morning, he asked her again if something was bothering her. She said she was just nervous, with the interview in a couple of hours. He kissed her, told her she was going to knock their socks off and got her to promise to call him as soon as she left IMI.

Once she was alone in his big house by the ocean, she took her time getting ready, making sure her hair and makeup were just right. She wore a gray pencil skirt and jacket to match, with a burnt-orange silk blouse underneath for the perfect pop of color. Sky-high taupe heels completed the outfit, a fabulous pair of shoes that still looked amazing five years after she'd bought them at Stuart Weitzman in New York. She'd had her mother get the outfit from her closet in Bozeman and overnight it to her in Rust Creek Falls so she could look her best.

The driver was waiting in front of the house. He took her straight to the IMI building on Century Park East. The man at the podium by the elevator took her name and sent her to the tenth floor. There, a beautiful receptionist led her to a small conference room.

Ten minutes later, she sat across from Carson's associate, Jason Velasco, two other ad executives and the top designer at the firm. After a minimum of cheerful chitchat, it got serious.

There was praise. They'd seen her work on her website and they were all impressed with her designs from the night of the moonshine. She might have laughed at that if she'd felt at all comfortable.

But she didn't feel comfortable, even though they thoroughly surprised her by telling her that Della Storm had a lot of good things to say about her.

Good things? Della? Really? She wasn't sure that she believed them. But then she thought about the letter she'd written and mailed last week. Could her apology have actually made a difference to Della?

Jason Velasco then cleared his throat and tiptoed into a mention of the "difficulties" of Tessa's last month with Della and the fact that she had been "terminated abruptly."

Tessa went with the "personal problems" explanation, keeping it general. There was nothing to be gained by getting specific. When they asked if those problems were resolved, she answered firmly that they were.

At the end, they thanked her and said they would be in touch. As Jason saw her to the elevator, he told her how much he loved working with Carson, as did everyone at IMI. He asked her to give Carson his best.

She promised that she would.

Again the car was waiting for her outside the building. As the driver took her back to Malibu, she stared out the tinted window and tried not to feel too discouraged.

Carson called when she was halfway there. "I thought you said you'd call me the minute you left IMI."

"Sorry. I was thinking about the interview, obsessing on it really."

"What happened? Are you okay?" He sounded so worried for her.

She got busy reassuring him. "I'm fine—I promise you. And I think it went pretty well."

"I know they'll make an offer."

They probably would. For his sake. That shouldn't have depressed her, but it did. She really didn't want to get a job because she happened to be sleeping with a powerful man. Somehow, that would be almost as bad as throwing over her career for one. "We'll see."

There was a lengthy silence on the line. Then finally he said, "Tessa, won't you tell me what's wrong?"

She lied and said, "Nothing," and hated herself for it. But really, were they going to discuss this now, on the phone?

No way. It had to wait till later.

She wasn't sure exactly when. But not right now.

He said he would be back at the house by five, and he was taking her out someplace nice to celebrate.

Celebrate what? she thought. *Ugh.* Surely she'd become the gloomiest person on the planet. "Can't wait," she replied, trying really hard to inject a little enthusiasm.

At Carson's house, she changed into the bikini she'd found in the cabana the day before, grabbed a towel, a bottle of sunscreen and a dog-eared paperback she'd taken from the sitting room at her grandma's boardinghouse and brought along to read on the plane. She swam several laps in the pool, slathered on the sunscreen and stretched out on a chaise with her book.

After an hour of reading, she wandered back inside

for lunch, then put on a beach cover-up and went down the stairs to the sand. She walked for two hours. When she returned to the house, she stretched out on Carson's California king.

He woke her right on time, at five, joining her in the bed for a while. That was good. Perfect even. If she could make love to Carson all day and night, she would never have to decide where her life was going.

Later, they went out to a gorgeous restaurant and ate on a wide deck in the glow of a thousand party lights, with a beautiful view of the ocean. He ordered an excellent cabernet and she had none of it.

He didn't ask her why—and he didn't ask her what was wrong. Apparently, he'd figured out by then that she wasn't going to tell him.

That night, she couldn't sleep. She crept quietly from his enormous bed, pulled on the filmy beach cover-up she'd left in the bathroom and went downstairs.

The pool deck shone silver in the moonlight. She pushed open the sliding door from the kitchen and went out.

A while later he found her there, sitting on the edge of the pool, her feet dangling in the water. "Are you ever going to talk to me?" He stood gazing down at her, wearing only a pair of track pants that rode low on his hard hips, the sculpted planes of his chest so beautiful in the moonlight. "Come on." He held out his hand.

She took it and let him pull her up into his waiting arms. "I'm sorry I'm such awful company. I just…need a little time. Everything's happening too fast, that's all."

He kissed her and then gazed down at her, unsmiling, a thousand questions in his eyes. "I can't make it right if you won't tell me what's wrong."

"That's just it. It's not your job to make it right. It's mine. And I...well, what I really need is to go home."

Surprisingly, he didn't argue. "When?"

"Tomorrow—or rather, today."

"I'll arrange for the plane. Rust Creek Falls or Bozeman?"

"Rust Creek Falls."

"Done. Come back to bed." He took her hand again and led her toward the glass doors. She followed him willingly up the stairs and climbed back beneath the covers with him, scooting close against him, her back to his broad chest. Really, she loved everything about him—the scent of his skin, the heat of him at her back, the strength in him. The will to win. His limitless confidence in his ability to mold the world to his liking. And his tenderness, too.

She just...wasn't ready; that was all. Not ready for the fabulous job he'd arranged for her. Not ready to decide which way her life should go. And definitely not ready to be having his baby.

Uh-uh. No way was she ready for that. If only her period would come. She would feel so much better about everything.

He wrapped his arm around her, smoothed her hair.

Eventually, she slept.

Carson had no damn clue what was going on with her.

He also didn't know how to find out what the problem was so they could work through it. She wasn't the least forthcoming lately. And asking got him nowhere. She'd shut him out.

The next morning they were careful with each other. He asked her to call him when she heard from IMI. She promised that she would, though she said nothing about when they might see each other again.

He didn't bring it up, either. Was he getting a little pissed at her? Oh, yes, he was.

But he was trying to be patient, an activity at which he'd never especially excelled. He was trying to give her time to come to him with the truth.

Whatever the hell that was.

He had a meeting at ten that he couldn't get out of. Her flight was set for noon, and he'd ordered a car to get her to the airport. He kissed her goodbye and left the house at nine.

At three that afternoon, he got a text from her. Home safe. Thanks for everything.

He had to actively resist the urge to throw his phone against the far wall of his office just to watch it shatter.

She wanted to play it cryptic? He could do that.

You're welcome, he texted back.

And nothing more.

Carson was angry with her. Tessa totally got that. She didn't blame him, either. She'd been cool and distant and completely uncommunicative, while he'd been charming and attentive and knocked himself out to make her LA visit a good one.

If only her period would come. As soon as it did, as soon as she knew there was no baby on the way, she would call him. They would work things out.

But her period didn't come. And she still had no idea what to say to him. So she didn't call. Or text. Or email. He returned the favor. There was a large and cold silence between them.

The weekend went by.

When Monday finally came, she couldn't stand it anymore. She went to Kalispell and bought a test, which she took first thing Tuesday morning.

Positive.

She stared at the little result window in complete disbelief. How was a positive result even possible? Okay, yes. She could see how it wouldn't have been wise to count on the condom wrappers they'd found the morning after the night of the moonshine. Not when they'd had no clear memory of what they'd actually done with the condoms themselves. One might have torn. Or maybe they'd been so out of it, they'd unwrapped them and then not bothered to use them.

Who could ever say?

But shouldn't she have been able to count on the morning-after pill, at least?

A little online research on that subject had her discovering the pill was about 95 percent effective if taken in the first twenty-four hours.

So, a 5 percent chance of failure.

Maybe the test had been wrong.

Wednesday, she took a second test. The result didn't change. Apparently, she'd somehow managed to fall into that lonely 5 percent.

Tessa sat at the window of her room at the boardinghouse and stared out over Cedar Street below.

A baby. She was having Carson's baby.

She was terrible with children. As for Carson, he'd made it much too clear that he didn't want children.

Where did that leave them?

Nowhere good.

She had no idea what to do, how to tell him. As she pondered the impossibility of breaking the big news to him, her phone rang.

It was Jason Velasco. "Tessa, hello!"

"Jason." It came out on a weary sigh.

"Is this a bad time?"

Terrible. "No. No, not at all." Somehow, she pulled it together and managed to inject at least a little enthusiasm. "What a...nice surprise. How are you doing?"

"Fine, fine." He told her about the weather in California, about the vacation he had coming up. He and his family were going to Hawaii.

And then he got down to it. He said he'd wanted to call her personally with IMI's offer, though human resources would be calling soon, too. The paperwork was on the way, all the terms laid out clearly, in detail.

He gave her the gist of it. She would be a full-fledged graphic designer, a midlevel position with an excellent salary, a generous benefit package and great potential for advancement.

As he chattered excitedly in her ear, a sort of calm settled over her.

She knew two things: She didn't want this job. And she was keeping her baby.

As soon as Jason paused for a breath, she told him where she stood. "I appreciate your calling me, Jason. I appreciate all the effort that you and your team put into making a place for me at IMI. But the truth is I just don't think we're a good fit."

Jason sputtered a bit, but he quickly recovered. He asked what her issues were, specifically, so that he could address them.

She stalled. "Exactly how frank would you like me to be?"

He didn't give up. "You feel...uncomfortable—is that it?"

"Yes. I know Carson pushed you to hire me. And you're right. I'm just not comfortable with that."

"Honestly, Tessa. You're clearly very talented. You impressed us. I really do feel you would make a great addition to our team."

"Well, thank you, Jason."

"So…how do I change your mind?"

"You don't. But I will definitely tell Carson how terrific you've been. I'll make it very clear to him that you, and everyone at IMI, have been helpful and welcoming. I'll let him know that the offer is excellent, but that it just doesn't work for me right now."

"You mean that." It wasn't a question.

"Yes. I do."

"What else can I say?"

"Nothing. Thank you again."

Jason let it go then. He wished her well and said goodbye.

After she hung up, she wondered if maybe she'd lost her mind to turn down a second chance at the big time. But it didn't really feel like she'd blown it. It felt more like the right choice, one that worked for her.

She should call Carson. She'd promised him that she would call as soon as she heard from IMI.

However, she had something a lot more important than a job offer to tell him about. And she couldn't make herself call him until she'd figured out what to say. And as for that, she had nothing.

Another day went by. Thursday she had an idea: maybe a letter. At the very least it might help to write down her thoughts, to plan out what to say to him.

She wrote the letter—or rather, an email. In it she told him she was pregnant and she was keeping the baby and she was sorry, but that was just how it was.

It was awful, that email. Whiny and wimpy. She

trashed it and tried again. That time, she opened with "I love you."

Ugh. Opening with "I love you" and moving right on to, "And I'm having your baby."

That somehow didn't work, either.

She tried writing it out on actual paper, the way she had the letter to Della. *Nope.* Putting it on paper didn't make it even one tiny bit better.

About then she had the blinding realization that telling a man you're having his baby was something you ought to have guts enough to do straight to his face.

So, okay. She needed to return to LA and speak with him in person. Probably the best plan was just to book a flight and go to him.

But that seemed all wrong. The poor man deserved at least a little warning. He didn't need her showing up on his doorstep out of the blue, babbling about love and babies.

Finally, on Friday, she made herself call him.

At least he picked up on the first ring. "Tessa. What a surprise." And not a happy one, judging by the ice-cold tone of his voice. "How are you?" Before she could decide how to answer that, he added, "I understand you turned down the job with IMI."

She winced and stifled a groan. "You, um, talked to Jason, then?"

"I did. And he talked to you...when was it?"

She let out a slow, careful breath. "Wednesday. And, yes, I promised I would call you. I'm sorry I didn't."

"You're sorry. Now, that really helps, Tessa. That makes me feel all warm and fuzzy inside."

"You're mad." She stated the obvious because she didn't know what else to say. "You're really, really mad."

"Figured that out, did you?"

She had so messed this up. Better, she decided, to cut to the point. "Look. I called because I...want to see you."

"Excellent," he muttered, ladling on the sarcasm. "I've got a few things I have to deal with here. Then I'll fly up there on Wednesday."

Her stomach lurched. "Did you just say you're coming back to Rust Creek Falls?" Hope bloomed within her. Bright, beautiful, ridiculous hope.

Hope for what, she wasn't sure.

But maybe he wasn't as finished with her as she'd thought.

"Yeah. Wednesday." He still sounded as cold as the dark side of the moon.

"Carson, are you sure? I'm happy to come there."

"Happy. Interesting word choice. No, I'll come to you."

She got the message. "You don't believe I'll actually show up, do you?"

"And what, I wonder, could possibly cause me to doubt that you'll do what you say you'll do?"

She was very close to yelling a few bad words into the phone and hanging up on him—because she knew he had a right to be mad at her and she didn't know what to do to make it better. She really, truly sucked at relationships. Women like her should not only *not* be allowed to get pregnant; they should never fall in love. People only got hurt when women like her fell in love.

"All right," she said at last. "See you Wednesday, then."

"Dinner," he growled at her. "I'll pick you up at seven. We'll go to that Italian place in Kalispell."

"Okay. That's good," she said. "I—I'm looking forward to seeing you and..." About then she realized she was talking to dead air.

He'd already hung up.

Chapter Eleven

Carson's plane landed in Kalispell at a few minutes past noon on Wednesday. He rented a car and headed for Rust Creek Falls, planning to go straight to the boardinghouse. So what if he was several hours early? He would surprise her. Maybe he'd catch her at a weak moment and she'd say something honest for a change.

He was still very angry at her. And he would probably say things to her that he'd regret later.

Well, too bad. There was no way he could wait until seven to see her. He'd already waited twelve never-ending damn days since she left him in Malibu. Because if she wanted to talk to him, she could damn well pick up the phone and call.

But she hadn't called. Until Friday.

And as of now, today, this moment, it was enough.

He was finding her immediately, and they were having it out. If it was over, he would damn well know sooner than later.

At the south end of town, he turned onto Main Street, headed north. He crossed the Main Street Bridge and saw a whole lot of red, white and blue up ahead. Coming even with the cluster of public buildings between the bridge and Cedar Street, he rolled by the library, all decked out in patriotic bunting. The town hall façade was the same—and the Community Center on the other side of the street, too.

Monday had been the Fourth of July. They must have left the decorations up.

Damn. He'd missed the parade. No doubt there had been babies involved, lots of flag-waving and veterans in uniform, chest candy glinting in the midday sun. True, he had no interest in small-town parades. Still, he felt strangely regretful that he'd missed the Rust Creek Falls version of the Fourth.

Did they have a barbecue in the park after the parade? Had Tessa been there?

He was so busy feeling left out and kicking himself mentally for even caring, that he was not the least prepared when Homer Gilmore suddenly materialized in the middle of the street waving his arms wildly, shouting, "Stop!"

Carson wasn't going very fast, but Homer had appeared out of nowhere. Carson hit the brakes, hard. Rubber squealed and burned as he slid to a stop a hair's breadth from mowing the old fool down.

"What the hell, Homer?" Carson yelled out his open driver's side window. "I could have killed you. Have you completely lost your mind?"

Homer didn't answer. And he didn't even look bothered that he'd almost become roadkill. Instead, he pointed a scrawny finger heavenward, as if to say, *Hold on a minute.*

Carson leaned on the horn.

Homer moved then—and fast, too. He darted around to the passenger door and tapped on the window.

Reluctantly, Carson rolled it down. "What?"

Homer stuck his head in. "We need to talk."

"No, we don't. It didn't go well with the moonshine that night."

"What's that mean, exactly?"

"It means that Drake Distilleries is having nothing to do with that stuff of yours. End of discussion."

Instead of replying, or pulling his head out of the window so that Carson could move on, Homer reached in and popped open the door.

"Homer, don't—" But Carson was too late.

The old miscreant had already hopped in. "Take me to the Ace in the Hole. I need a burger. And we still need to talk."

Someone honked. Carson checked the rearview mirror to see that a quad cab pulling a horse trailer had stopped behind him. The driver honked again.

"Let's go." Homer made a shooing motion with his left hand as he hooked the seat belt with his right. "You can't just park yourself in the middle of Main Street, blocking other people's way."

At the Ace in the Hole, Homer insisted on a quiet booth in the back. "So's we can talk business private-like." He ordered a double-decker cheeseburger with fries and a beer.

Carson hadn't eaten since before he'd left the house in Malibu that morning, so he went ahead and ordered the same. "Now what?" he asked the old man once their waitress had brought them their beers.

Homer took a pull off his longneck and set it down hard. He burped good and loud. "I needed that."

Carson tried again, speaking slowly, as one would to a child. Or an idiot. "Did you hear what I said back there on Main Street, Homer? I'm not interested in your moonshine formula anymore."

Narrowing his reddened eyes and bunching up his grizzled eyebrows, Homer leaned across the table. "You tellin' me you didn't have the best night of your life that night?"

Carson scoffed. "I'm not telling you anything of the sort. I can't even remember what happened that night. That moonshine of yours causes blackouts, Homer. I had one. And so did Tessa. That is dangerous stuff. You're lucky no one's sued you yet—not to mention, had you arrested."

"Arrested? For what?"

"I don't know. Running a moonshine still without a distilled spirits permit? Or maybe just plain drugging people?"

Homer drew his scrawny shoulders back and announced with a sniff, "Everybody who drinks my 'shine does so of his or her own free will."

Now Carson was the one leaning across the scratched table between them. "Don't give me that. I've heard the stories. You spiked the wedding punch a year ago, on the Fourth. The people who drank it then had no idea what they were in for."

Homer took another swallow of his beer. He set the bottle down more gently that time. "I just wanted 'em to loosen up, you know? Make connections, have some fun."

Carson opened his mouth with a comeback. But what was the point? He might as well argue with the wall. "Whatever excuses you want to make for yourself, at least get clear on the fact that I'm *not* buying your moonshine formula."

Homer's eyes lit up as he stared past Carson's shoulder. "Oh, look. Here come our burgers."

The waitress served them. When she left, Homer dug in. Carson ate, too, his mind on Tessa, on what she might be doing right now. He hoped she would be at the boardinghouse when he finally ditched Homer and got over there.

The old man demolished his meal in no time flat, finishing up the first beer and ordering a second one. Finally, he wiped his mouth with his napkin and pushed his plate away. "Nothin' like a burger and a beer, I always say."

"Homer, are we clear, then? I'm not buying your moonshine. There will be no deal."

Homer only grinned wide, showing off those yellowed teeth that had never made the acquaintance of a competent orthodontist. "I do like your style, Carson Drake. And I just need a few more weeks to decide for sure if I can work with you."

About then, Carson realized that trying to get on the same page with Homer Gilmore was an exercise in futility. The old guy lived in his own world on his own terms. "Whatever you say, Homer." He put his concentration where it would do some good: on eating his burger and enjoying his fries.

And then Homer asked in a very serious tone, "So, what do you think about the situation with Tessa?"

The old guy was more than a little creepy. At that moment, Carson almost felt that Homer could see into his brain. Carson answered warily, "I...like Tessa. Very much."

Homer waved a bony hand. "I didn't ask if you *liked*

her. I asked how you're doing with her having your baby and when are the two of you steppin' up and makin' it legal? That's what I asked."

What the...?

Carson choked down a last bite of burger and pushed his own plate away. "Who told you that Tessa is pregnant?"

Homer thought that was funny, apparently. He chortled. "Nobody told me. Nobody *had* to tell me. You both had my moonshine, didn't you? And everybody knows what happens when a man and a woman drink my moonshine together."

The sudden knot in Carson's stomach untied itself. Tessa wasn't pregnant. Homer was just being Homer. The old coot had probably been sampling his own product.

"Well?" Homer demanded.

Carson leaned forward again and pinned Homer with a cold glare. "You don't know what you're talking about, old man. And you should know better than to go spreading stories you made up in your head."

Homer gave a slow and weirdly satisfied nod. "You're protective of that sweet girl. That's a good thing. A man should be protective of his woman." He leaned in, too, until his road map of a face was only inches from Carson's. "And I don't carry no tales," he muttered on a beery breath. "This here conversation, it's just between us. Strictly man-to-man. You can walk out of here dead certain that I will never share your private business with another living soul. Now, if you'll excuse me, I need to see a man about a horse."

Homer got up and followed the signs to the men's room. Carson paid the bill and finished his beer, his impatience growing as the minutes ticked by and the old man failed to reappear. The guy was not only a menace to society with his dangerous moonshine and his tendency to pop up out of bushes and materialize out of nowhere in the middle of the street; he was downright rude. Carson should just get up and go. It wasn't as if he'd even wanted this impromptu meeting with the old reprobate.

Finally, he decided he could use a trip to the men's room himself. He got up and went in there.

Empty. *Of course.*

He took care of business. On the way out, he asked the waitress if she'd seen where Homer went.

She shook her head. "Sorry. I never saw him leave your booth."

Five minutes later, Carson parked on the street in front of Strickland's Boarding House and marched up to the front door.

Old Gene answered his knock. "Hey." Gene wore a wide smile. Whatever might be going on with Tessa and whatever Old Gene knew about it, he seemed to have no issue with Carson. "How you doin', son?"

The tension between Carson's shoulder blades eased a little. "Great, thanks."

"Lookin' for Tessa?" Old Gene ushered him in. "She's down in the basement on laundry duty."

And just like that, Carson was heading down the back stairs. He found her at the folding table busy with a tall pile of towels. Both of the dryers and the two washers were going, making enough noise that she hadn't heard him coming. She just went on folding, her back to him, completely unaware of his presence.

His footsteps slowed at the sight of her. He paused at the base of the stairs, his heart roaring in his chest, his belly tight, burning with a potent mix of frustration and yearning. She wore Chuck Taylors, torn, faded jeans that clung to her fine butt and a striped tank with a neck so wide, it had fallen down her arm one side to reveal the soft curve of her shoulder. Her hair was piled in a sloppy bun at the top of her head, wild curls escaping in little corkscrews along the back of her neck.

His heart rate slowed to a steady, hungry rhythm and the burning in his gut became something closer to arousal than anger. It was the best he'd felt in days.

"Tessa."

Her slim shoulders stiffened. She dropped the hand towel she'd just grabbed and whirled to face him, those dark eyes taking him in, that wide mouth not quite knowing whether to smile or to scowl. "Carson."

The sound of his name on her lips broke the spell that held him rooted in place. Yeah, they really needed to talk. But more than that, he had to have his hands on her.

In five long strides, he eliminated the distance between them, reaching for her as she grabbed for him. He lifted her, and she jumped right up into his waiting arms, wrapping those slim legs good and tight around his waist, plastering her sweet self against the front of him.

She was on him like a barnacle, her hands in his hair, those lips he needed so badly to taste hovering just out of reach. "You're early," she whispered, wonderfully breathless with what just might be a longing equal to his own. *God.* She smelled so good, sweet and fresh, like rain and flowers and fabric softener.

"We have to talk." He growled the words at her.

She cradled his face between her two small hands. "I know. Yes. I know we do."

He couldn't wait a minute longer to have her mouth on his. She must have felt the same. Because her soft lips came crashing down, closing on his with a whimper of need.

So good. Incomparable. Tessa's hot little mouth moving on his, her sweet tongue spearing in, warring with his, her arms closing tighter, her body pressing closer.

When she tried to lift her mouth away, he reached up a hand, his fingers spread wide to cup the back of her head. He guided her back to him, taking her mouth again.

The second kiss tasted even better than the first. He held her firmly in place and plundered her mouth for all he was worth, lowering her to the folding table as he kissed her, laying her out onto the warm pile of towels.

Finally, when she pushed a little at his shoulders and wiggled in his hold with growing resistance, he lifted up enough to look at her, at her mouth all swollen from his kisses, her hair tumbling down, coming loose from that topknot, her eyes dazed and dreamy. "I need an hour," she said breathlessly, "to finish up the laundry."

He stroked a hand down her arm, along the gorgeous curve of her hip. Holding her gaze, he demanded, "Then we talk."

"Yes."

"No blowing me off this time."

She shook her head. "I swear." She reached up, pressed her cool, smooth hand to his cheek. Damn, he had missed her—those gold-flecked, coffee-brown eyes, the sweet and husky sound of her voice, the gentle touch of her hand. Everything. All of her. "One hour," she vowed. "And we'll talk."

He helped her fold the towels and sheets. They worked together silently, all the things that needed saying hanging in the humid basement air between them. He had about a thousand questions—most of them beginning with the word *why*.

For now, though, he didn't ask even one of them. No

point in getting into it until they could be alone, with no chance of interruption.

Between loads, they went upstairs together and visited with Melba and Claire in the kitchen. Melba asked him how long he would be in town this time.

He cut a quick glance at Tessa. Their gazes caught and locked. He knew she was waiting for his answer—an answer he couldn't give right then. "Not sure. It depends."

"Will you be needing a room?" Melba asked next.

He'd already reserved his former suite at the Manor. But he might want a room at the boardinghouse, too, depending on what happened when he and Tessa were alone. "Still got the room next to Tessa's?"

Melba set down her coffee cup and rose from the table. "Been saving it for you."

Tessa's eyes widened at her grandmother's words, but she didn't comment.

Melba led him to the office, where he took that room for the rest of the month. If things went badly with Tessa, he might never set foot in it. But if he wanted it, he would have it. Never hurt to keep his options open.

It was after four when he helped Tessa fold the last sheet.

Then she said, "Come upstairs to my room."

"Not here," he replied. The boardinghouse was a second home to her. Her sister or one of her grandparents might come tapping on the door at any time. No. He wanted her on his turf. "Let's go to the Manor. We can talk in the suite. No one will bother us there."

She regarded him so seriously. He had no idea what might be going on behind those fine brown eyes. "Okay. I'll just grab my purse."

At Maverick Manor, in the sitting room of his suite, she took the sofa. He started to sit beside her, but she put up a hand. "Would you sit across from me? I want to be…face-to-face."

Was that a bad sign?

Lately, with her, he just didn't know.

His gut knotting up again, the muscles between his shoulder blades drawing tight, he took the club chair across the coffee table from her. "All right. We're face-to-face." *Now, what the hell is going on with you?*

"I…" She gripped the sofa cushions on either side of her, as though to ground herself. "I'm sorry I didn't call you when I turned down the job with IMI. I should have."

He did want to talk about what had happened with IMI. Still, he had the strangest feeling that she'd just detoured from the main subject. Whatever that subject might actually be. But fine. He had plenty to say with regard to the job at IMI. "You said you would call."

"Yeah, I know. And I apologize."

"But why didn't you?" He kept his tone as soft and even as he could manage. "Am I that hard to talk to?"

"No," she said instantly. And then, "Yes." And then, "I think I mentioned before how it's all happening so fast with us. And I, well, I've been feeling kind of over-whelmed. I told you I'm no good at this, at trying to make a relationship work." Now she seemed flustered, and she rushed to add, "I mean, if a relationship is what we have, though I suppose it's too early to get real specific as to what exactly to call this thing with us, and I…" She was clutching the cushions again. "Oh, God. I'm making no sense, none at all."

He almost laughed. "On second thought, forget about why."

Her eyes softened. And so did that mouth he was long-ing to kiss. "You mean that?"

"Yeah. It's all right. You're sorry you didn't call, and

I accept your apology. Let's leave it there." He really wanted to touch her, to hold her. But she was over there, and he was over here. He needed to rectify that problem, and soon.

And then, miracle of miracles, she held out her hand. "I know I asked you to sit over there. But would you come here? Please?"

He wrapped his fingers around hers, got up and scooted around the table to join her on the couch. With a sigh, she swayed against him. He gathered her close, pressed his lips against her hair. "I still have questions."

A small sigh escaped her. "Go ahead."

"Did Jason or his team give you a hard time about how your job with the Storm woman ended?"

She stiffened and drew away. "Absolutely not. They really did plan to hire me and Jason was… I like him. He called me personally to tell me I had the job. It was a good offer. And when I turned it down, he made a real effort to change my mind. We did speak of it, of course, of Della, but she wasn't the issue. I promise you."

"So then, what was the issue?" He suspected that LA was the problem, that having to live there was a complete deal-breaker for her.

If so, where did that leave them? He would do a lot to be with her, but he needed to be in LA much of the year to run the Drake companies effectively. Relocating to the wilds of Montana wasn't going to cut it for him— even if he had grown strangely fond of Rust Creek Falls.

"The truth is, Carson…" She faltered again, scooting farther away from him and grabbing for the sofa cushions. "I really don't want a job that I get because you want me to have it. I don't want a job I get on your say-so because my new boss wants to keep you happy."

So, then, in spite of what she'd said a minute ago, Jason

and crew *did* mess it up. If so, heads would roll. Carson asked in a carefully neutral tone, "What you're saying is they made it clear to you that they were only hiring you because *I* wanted you hired."

Her dark eyes flashed. She tapped one of her Chuck Taylors impatiently. "Of course not. I've told you. They were gracious and perfectly reasonable and they never said any such thing. Still, we all knew exactly what was going on."

"Which was?"

"Seriously, Carson. How many ways do I have to explain this?"

"What I'm saying is, even given that I instigated the process, they *wanted* to hire you. I just don't get it. Where is the problem?"

"I told you the problem. I want to find my own damn job."

"And you did."

She shot him a narrow-eyed glance, then instantly looked away. "I have no idea what you're talking about."

"Look at this logically. You just said that IMI made you a bona fide offer, that they wanted to hire you. So you did it. You found a great job. All I did was get the ball rolling. Because face it—even *I* couldn't get you hired if you weren't going to be able to do the job."

"Please. You so could. And I don't want that. I don't want you to get me a job. I want to get my *own* job. Yes, I'm stumbling around in the dark about this, having a hard time finding my way. But still, I need to do this my way, for myself."

"I think you're being naive."

Her sweet mouth thinned to a hard line. "Thank you so much for your input."

He tried to make light of it. "Ouch. The sarcasm is killing me."

Hectic spots of color flamed high on her cheeks. "Let's make a deal. You stop treating me like a silly little woman and I'll control my sarcasm."

"I was not—"

"Yes, Carson. You were." She was looking right at him now. It wasn't a happy look. For a long count of five, she glared at him and he tried to figure out what to say next that wouldn't have her bouncing to her feet and heading for the door.

Because she mattered to him. A whole lot.

It was of paramount importance to him that somehow they work this out. That she not give up on him.

On them.

All he'd wanted for years was his freedom, to taste every delight life had to offer. He worked hard and played hard. It had been great.

But now there was Tessa with her dark gypsy eyes and her wide mouth made for kissing, with her sharp mind and guarded heart. Now freedom didn't look all that wonderful, frankly. Freedom just felt like loneliness.

Now he really needed to figure out how to keep her from walking away.

Finally, she spoke. "I'm going to say all this one more time, and you'd better be listening. Jason and the team at IMI treated me well, with courtesy and professional respect. It's not their fault that I'm not going to work for them. I said no to their offer, and I'm glad that I did. It was the right choice for me. I regret that I didn't keep my word and call you about it. That's on me, and I'll do better next time."

He took her hand. When she didn't instantly jerk away, he considered that a good sign. "Okay."

She swallowed hard. "Okay, what?"

He rubbed the back of her hand with his thumb, loving the feel of her, skin to skin, wanting to kiss her, wondering how long he would have to wait before she let him. Was he totally whipped? It kind of appeared so. "Okay, the job wasn't right for you and you need to run your own career without interference from me."

"That's it, yes. If I want your help, I'll ask for it—and then you can decide if you even want to help me." At least she said that kind of tenderly.

"Of course I'll help you any way I can." The words came out raw sounding, rough with emotion. He made his confession. "I'm a complete fool for you, Tessa."

The sweetest, softest sigh escaped her. "You are not in any way a fool."

"Oh, yeah, I am. For you, I am. It's been crap in LA without you. You're what I think about. You're what I want." He reeled her in.

And she let him, thank heaven.

Damn, he was starved for the taste of her. He wrapped his arms around her and lowered his mouth to hers.

The kiss was long and deep and thorough, and Tessa reveled in it.

When he eased his hand up under her shirt, she didn't stop him. Far from it. She moaned in invitation and pushed her breast into his palm.

When he took her shirt away and unhooked her bra, she loved it. When he unzipped her old jeans and guided her to her feet so he could slide them down to a pool of tattered denim around her ankles, she loved that, too.

He went to his knees on the rug. She stared down at his dark head as he untied her shoes. At his command, she stepped out of them.

Next he took down her satin boy shorts with the lace inserts on the sides. And then he pressed his mouth to the hot, feminine core of her and did things to her that probably ought to be illegal.

She combed her fingers through his hair, clutching him to her, whispering his name, knowing herself for a dishonest coward—and crying out in pure joy anyway as she came.

Later. The word whispered through her mind as she pulled him to his feet and stripped off his shirt, so eager to get to his bare skin that buttons went flying.

Later, I'll tell him. We'll go to dinner. I'll tell him then, just as I planned.

But now…

Well, now she was the one going down to her knees. She took him in her mouth, loving the salty taste of him, taking him so deep, sliding her tongue along the thick vein that ran the length of him, until he moaned her name and fisted his hands in her hair.

When he pulled her up, threw her over his shoulder and headed for the bedroom, she laughed and kicked her feet and pretended to protest. And then he put her down so carefully on the bed, as though she were precious, fragile. Breakable.

She didn't let herself even think that she should tell him the truth about the baby first and take her pleasure later. When he rolled on a condom, she didn't say a word about how they no longer needed one—well, at least not for contraception.

She just opened for him and pulled him into her yearning arms and let the wonder roll through her, let his slow, hot, skilled caresses obliterate her until she was only a conduit for each thrilling sensation. Twice more, she came. It was magnificent.

And when she finally felt him pulsing within her, she gloried in it.

Later, she thought, when she held him close afterward. *I'll tell him at dinner, just as I planned.*

At the Italian place in Kalispell, they got the same booth they'd had the time before—in a quiet little corner where they could talk without being disturbed. She joked with him that it was so nice be back at "their" Italian place.

He agreed. "We need to come here often."

She wondered how they would do that, with him living in LA. But then, maybe *she* would move to LA, too, and they would find a favorite Italian place there.

Maybe it would actually work out between them. She could find freelance work much more easily in LA. They would live together and raise their baby together, and maybe find a little getaway place of their own in Rust Creek Falls. They could visit a few times a year.

Maybe.

Or maybe not.

Maybe that was all just a crazy fantasy.

Who could say?

The first step was to tell him.

And she hadn't even gotten there yet.

But she didn't let all those maybes show in her expression. She only laughed and said, "Yes. We should come here to 'our' Italian place at least once a week."

She ordered veal, and he had the chicken Parmesan. When he poured her a glass of Chianti, she didn't stop him, though that would have been a good lead-in to breaking the news she should have shared hours ago. She let him pour the wine, and she never touched the glass.

If he noticed, he didn't let on.

He talked about Drake Distilleries, about the terrific ad campaign IMI had developed for an all new product line of flavored liqueurs. And Drake Hospitality would soon be opening a new club in San Diego. He said he wanted to take her to the big first-night party at the end of August. She said she would love that, though August seemed a million years away and she thought to herself that anything could happen by then.

He didn't even *want* children.

How could this possibly end well?

Panic jittered through her.

She quelled it and reported that she'd picked up more work through her website and, yes, there had been a parade along Main Street on the Fourth of July. "It was strangely similar to the one on Memorial Day."

"I'll bet. Barbecue in the park afterward?"

"How did you guess?"

He gave a low, sexy chuckle. "What's Independence Day in Rust Creek Falls without a parade and a barbecue after?"

"It was fun," she said. And then confessed, "I wished you were here."

He set down his wineglass. "Me, too." He said it quietly. And his dark eyes seemed to say she was the only other person in the world right then.

Just the two of them, together. It could work. She knew it could.

Except that it *wasn't* just the two of them.

Because baby made three.

He smiled at her, a musing kind of smile.

She asked, "What?"

And he said, "I think I'm starting to like it in Rust Creek Falls. Ryan said it would happen. I hate when he's right."

The waitress served the main course.

Carson dug into his chicken parm and started telling her about how he'd run into Homer before he came looking for her at the boardinghouse. "I'm serious," he insisted. "Literally, I *ran* into Homer—or almost, anyway. He popped up out of nowhere in the middle of Main Street. I barely hit the brakes in time to keep from plowing him down. He wanted a burger and to talk about his moonshine. So I took him to the Ace in the Hole and tried to tell him that the moonshine deal was off. He refused to hear me, just kept saying he needed another few weeks to make up his mind. It only got weirder."

"Knowing Homer, I can't say I'm surprised." She twirled up a bite of linguini.

"He asked me how the 'situation' was with you."

"That's a strange way to put it."

"I thought so, too. And then he said he knew you were pregnant and what was I going to do about that?"

She froze with her forkful of linguini halfway to her mouth. Her face must have said it all.

Because Carson was suddenly watching her way too closely, eyes sharp and assessing.

Her hand was shaking. Slowly, she lowered her fork to her plate.

He suggested, way too gently, "Right now would be a great time to reassure me that it's not true."

Chapter Twelve

Carson waited for her to laugh and tell him that he really shouldn't jump to conclusions.

But she didn't laugh. She just went on staring at him through wide, haunted eyes, her linguine-wrapped fork abandoned on her plate.

Finally, in a voice that came out sounding way more freaked than he meant it to, he demanded, "It's true, then?"

Those thick dark lashes lowered. He watched her draw a careful breath and then let it out with agonizing slowness. Finally, she looked at him again. "Yes. It's true." She said the words flatly. Quietly.

Still, they echoed in his head like a shout. "But I don't…" He had no idea what he was trying to say. He took another crack at it. "So it was the night of the moonshine? You're saying Homer had it right?" He still couldn't believe it.

"Yes."

How was this even possible? He struggled to process. "But…the condoms, the morning-after pill…"

One slim shoulder lifted in a sad little half shrug. And then she craned across the booth toward him and insisted in a hot, angry whisper, "I did take that pill. I swear I did."

"Whoa. Hold on."

"What do you mean, hold on?" She was still whispering, but each word came out sharp and furiously clear. "I didn't ask for this, Carson. I did everything in my power to prevent it—well, except *not* to drink Homer's moonshine. I really should have thought twice before I did that."

"Stop. Listen. I'm not blaming you for getting pregnant. I believe you took that pill."

"Then why did you say—"

He cut her off with a wave of his hand. "Look. It's kind of a shock, okay?"

She sagged back into the red pleather seat. "Well, all right. I hear that." She picked up her fork—and then put it back down again. It clattered against her plate. "Suddenly I don't feel much like eating."

Neither did he. And he had a question he had to get an answer to. "Were you ever planning to tell me?"

"Of course."

He was far from convinced. "When?"

She winced—and made her answer into another question. "Over dessert?"

"Dessert," he echoed, remembering all the days she hadn't called him, recalling the day just past, when she'd kissed him and held him and they'd had it out over the job at IMI. So many chances she'd had to tell him.

And she hadn't.

"Carson, I…" She started to reach out. He stiffened,

not ready for her touch, not willing to be soothed by her. She saw him flinch and dropped her hand. "I promise you, I was getting to it. I really was."

"Getting to it how?"

"I'm not really sure. But I was working up to it. I *was*."

He drank some more Chianti, noticing for the first time that her glass was still full. And come to think of it, what about that champagne she wouldn't drink in LA the evening after the interview with IMI? And what about the way she just stopped talking to him then, no matter how hard he knocked himself out to convince her to let him in? "You've known since LA," he accused.

"I—"

"Don't you lie to me, Tessa. Don't you dare."

"Fine. All right, I suspected something then. My period was late. But I didn't take a test until I got home."

He just shook his head. "I thought we'd really made progress. I thought you were finally opening up to me today when we talked about that damn job you wouldn't take with IMI. I thought we were getting down to the crap that really matters. And then I took you to bed." He couldn't get over that. "We went to bed—and still you didn't tell me."

"Carson, I—"

"Do you trust me at all?"

"I'm trying."

"Uh-uh. Wait a minute." He jabbed an index finger in her direction. "This is it, isn't it? This is the real reason you didn't call me when you turned down the IMI job. This is the real reason you finally did call. You're holding all the information, and I'm in the dark, sitting here thinking how we've gotten past a rough patch and now I'm feeling so close to you…"

"I didn't blow you off. I was just waiting for the right time, that's all."

"From my side of the table, Tessa, I can see a long series of right times, none of which you took. On the contrary, you waited. You saved it up to tell me in a restaurant, in public, instead of earlier when at least we were alone and didn't have to have this out in whispers."

Her soft mouth trembled. She drew herself up. "All right. Yes, I should have gotten to it sooner. I made it seem like my issue was only about the job with IMI, just like you said. I made you think we'd worked through the problem when I hadn't even told you the real problem. And then, well, you kissed me and I kissed you and all I wanted was to be with you, to make love with you and forget about the future and how to tell you that there was a baby—about how and when and where to go from here. Okay, maybe getting to it here at the restaurant was a bad choice. But I wouldn't have let the night go by without telling you. It's why I called you and said we needed to talk. It's huge and I know it and I…well, now it's all blown up in my face. But you really do need to know everything."

He jerked up straight, every nerve at attention. "What the hell. There's *more*?"

"Stop looking at me like that. I just mean you should also know I'm keeping this baby. I want this baby no matter how bad a mother I'm going to turn out to be and—" She made a soft little sound, something midway between a moan and whimper. "God. I don't know. What else is there to say right now? I'm pregnant and I'm keeping it and that's about the size of it."

He could not sit there for one second longer. Not without picking up his plate and throwing his half-finished chicken Parmesan at the empty booth across the way. He slapped his napkin onto the table and slid from the booth. "Do not move. I'll be right back."

"Carson, please try to—"

"I need a minute."

"Carson—"

He didn't want to hear it, refused to hang around and listen to her next excuse. He turned his back on her and headed for the men's room.

There was nobody in there. *Thank God for small favors.* He splashed water on his face and stared at himself in the mirror over the sinks.

"A father…" He blinked at himself in disbelief and then scoffed at his dripping face. "You. A dad." He swore low, a string of harsh words, as he whipped a few paper towels from the dispenser and wiped the water off.

He'd never planned to be a dad.

But then, he hadn't planned on Tessa, either. He was one of those guys who'd thought he'd learned his lesson when his marriage failed. He'd spent years purposely never getting all that deeply involved.

Until Tessa.

One look at her and not getting involved went right out the window. Insta-love, insta-lust. Whatever it was, he'd known at the first sight of her that she was a game changer.

But a kid?

He hadn't bargained on a kid. He tossed the towels in the trash bin and stared at himself in the mirror some more as the shock of it faded.

Yeah, he was still seriously pissed at her for the way she'd handled this.

Which was *not* to handle it at all.

But he was also starting to get that itchy feeling at

the back of his neck, the one that told him he'd behaved badly.

Worse than badly.

Like a complete ass.

He'd let his anger get the better of him. She hadn't trusted him on so many levels, had been living with this secret for at least a couple of weeks now. He'd known there was a problem, had done everything but beg her to confide in him.

Still, she'd kept it from him. And that really got to him. For the first time in years, he wanted more than a good time from a woman. He wanted her to talk to him, to trust in him. But she hadn't.

And that made him want to break something big and heavy—something that would make a lot of noise as it shattered.

It really wasn't like him, to lose it like this. He ran a string of successful companies. He knew how to keep himself in check.

Except, apparently, when it came to Tessa.

Tessa and their baby.

Our baby.

My God.

He bent over the sink again and splashed more cold water on his face, dried off for the second time and raked his hair in place with his fingers. Then he retucked his shirt and straightened his jacket.

Ready as he'd ever be—which was to say, not ready at all.

But he had to get back to her. He wouldn't put it past her to get up and walk out. Because she'd screwed up by not telling him, by lying about it and insisting that noth-ing was wrong. And he'd been a jerk when the truth finally came out. Who knew what she thought of him right at this moment?

Parents. They were going to be parents. God help the poor kid.

He hadn't realized he'd been holding his breath until he came out of the hallway from the men's room and saw that she was still in the booth. *Good.* He got over there fast and slid in across from her.

But his moment of relief didn't last. The first words out of her mouth were, "I've had enough for tonight, Carson. Please take me back to the boardinghouse now."

He quelled the urge to argue. She looked tired, worn-out. And he needed some time to process all this, time to figure out how to work through this with her. He might be shocked all to hell to learn he was going to be a father, but she'd been carrying the burden of that truth for weeks now. *She* was the pregnant one, the one who needed a little tender care and understanding—neither of which he'd provided so far.

"Tessa, I—"

She didn't let him finish. "Please. No more tonight. I just can't take it right now."

Carson spent that night alone in his suite at Maverick Manor. He never went to bed. He watched bad late-night television without paying attention.

And he thought about Tessa and the baby and what he would do.

By morning, everything was clear. He got online and chose a ring, then called his assistant at home. She promised to get the ring from Cartier and get it to him overnight. The size would probably be wrong, but he could have it fixed in a matter of a day or two. If he was taking a knee, it seemed important that there *be* a ring, and a gorgeous one, even if it didn't quite fit.

Once the ring was handled, he called Tessa. She answered, which he decided to take as a good sign.

"Hi." Her voice was soft, a little sleepy. Something inside him ached in a way that was both painful and sweet. "You're up early."

"I didn't sleep. I've been thinking."

"Yeah." She made a soft sound—a sigh, a stifled yawn? "It's a lot to take in—I know."

"I want to see you. I promise not to be an ass."

Another sound that might have been a husky little chuckle. God, he hoped so. "Good to know. And yeah. We still need to talk."

"How about breakfast? If you come here, there's room service." He braced to be more convincing when she said no.

But then she said, "Half an hour, I'll be there."

"I'll order ahead. What do you want?"

"Poached eggs and toast and maybe some fresh fruit?"

"You got it."

She smiled when he opened the door, a weary little smile. He wanted to pull her close for a kiss, stroke her hair, rub her back. But that seemed wrong, somehow, after all that had gone down the night before. They needed to make up officially, before there could be kissing.

Didn't they?

The food arrived a couple of minutes after she did. The living area of the suite had a table with four chairs. They sat there. He spooned eggs Benedict into his mouth, hardly tasting it, not knowing how to begin.

This was hard. Wanting her so much, knowing from

the first that she was someone special. And yeah, okay, they both had issues, but didn't everybody? He'd set his sights on working through them. And then it had all gone wrong so suddenly when she stopped talking to him during her visit to LA. Yesterday, he'd just started to let himself think they were getting somewhere.

And then he found out about the baby.

Everything felt backward. They should have had more time to find their way as a couple before something like this happened. Neither of them had been thinking about having kids.

In fact, as he recalled, they'd both agreed that they were hopeless with babies—which was just fine because neither of them planned to have any.

Damn Homer Gilmore and his magic moonshine. Damn him to hell and back.

She spooned up berries from her fruit bowl—and then dropped them back in the bowl again. "Carson, I feel so terrible about all of this."

"Don't," he said, taking care, as he hadn't the night before, to speak gently, to use an affectionate tone. "Don't feel terrible. Just eat. Then we'll talk." He braced for her comeback.

But there wasn't one. She stuck her spoon back in the berries and got to work finishing her meal.

Twenty minutes later, they moved to the seating area. She took the sofa. He got the club chair.

Just like yesterday.

Today it was his turn to open with an apology. "I really was a jerk last night. I'm sorry."

She gave him a gentle smile and proceeded to be a lot more gracious than he'd been. "It's all right. It was a shocker, and I made a mess of telling you—or *not* telling you I guess is more accurate. But it's done now. You know about the baby. We can move on. And I, well, honestly, Carson. You don't have to worry."

He frowned at her. "I should be worried?"

"Well, I mean, I wouldn't blame you for wondering if I'm after your money."

He let out a sharp bark of laughter. "Come on. You wouldn't even let me find you a great job. You're the most independent woman I know. Not to mention you've got an excess of foolish pride."

"I'm only saying that I don't expect anything of you—I promise."

I don't expect anything. He didn't like the sound of that. "That's garbage. You damn well should expect things of me. You should expect *everything* of me." He said it a little more forcefully than he meant to.

She fiddled with the collar of the silky blue shirt she wore. "Well, fine. You seem pretty sure of all this. What *should* I expect of you? What does 'everything' mean?"

He reminded himself to speak quietly, reasonably. "I can tell you what *I* expect."

"Thank you. Please do."

"I want to take care of you. I want us to be together. That's what *I* expect, and you damn well should, too."

She looked at him sideways. "Together as in...?"

He'd jumped ahead. He knew he had. He shouldn't be saying this today. He needed to wait for the ring, at least. And a better understanding between them probably wouldn't hurt, either. Right now, they were just supposed to be healing the wounds they'd dealt each other yesterday and the two weeks before that. "Okay, I'm rushing things."

She hugged her arms around herself. "Carson, I'm not following."

He hated the damn coffee table. Twice now it had

stood between them. He rose. "Come over here." When she only gazed up at him, bewildered, he reached across and captured her wrist. She allowed him to take it, though somewhat reluctantly. "Over here." He tugged her up off the cushions and led her to the center of the room where no furniture was in the way. As soon as he had the space for it, he dropped to one knee.

By then, she knew what was coming. "Oh, Carson." Her mouth twisted as she stared down at him.

He should knock this off. Now. But it just wasn't in him to back down at this point. He had to take a crack at getting a yes out of her up front, at cutting through all the yada yada and sealing the deal. Once he got her commitment, they could work through all the rest. "Marry me, Tessa. You're all I think about. You're all I want. I'm crazy for you—and yeah. I know it's fast. I know it's scary. I know if I said that I loved you right now, you probably wouldn't believe me. So I won't say it, okay? I won't say it yet. But won't you just take a chance on me? If you'll only say yes, we can make it work. I know we can."

For a moment, he actually thought he'd done it. He knew she would say yes.

But then she dropped to *her* knees in front of him, which put her as close to eye to eye with him as possible, given his extra height. Now they knelt together in the center of the room.

"Tessa?" he asked, as she took his face between her hands. He didn't think he liked where this was going somehow. But it did feel good, her soft palms against his skin. Her cheeks had gone bright pink, and her eyes gleamed with what might have been tears.

Or, just possibly, laughter.

"You haven't mentioned the baby," she whispered downright tenderly.

"The baby." It came out gruff. "Of course, the baby. That's why we need to get this going, get it together. We need to be married so we can deal with all our crap and be ready to be actual parents when the baby comes."

She feathered her fingers along the hair at his temples. That felt terrific. What she said next? Not so much. "You've mentioned more than once that you never wanted children."

He turned his face into her hand and pressed a kiss to the heart of her palm. "And you've said the same to me."

"Not my point."

He was starting to get irritated. "There's a point?"

"Yes, Carson. The baby is the point. I don't really think you're ready for this…to marry me when you've barely known me a month because we're having a baby when you don't even *want* a baby."

"How about you let *me* be the judge of what I'm ready for? I want to marry you. We can work it all out."

"I just don't think it's that simple. As things stand now, I'm ready for you to be however involved you want to be. You didn't sign up for this, and I understand that. I can totally accept your not really being there for our child."

"What are you talking about? I *want* to be there."

"I'm saying that if we were married, I'd have higher expectations of you, and our child would, too."

"Fine. Good. I already told you. You should have expectations. So should the kid. Bring them the hell on."

"If we were married," she kept on way too patiently, "I would expect you to be a hands-on father, to be involved with our child."

"Involved. Fine. I can do that."

She let her caressing hands fall to her sides with a tired

sigh. "Carson, you don't even like children." She got up and stood gazing down at him until he began to feel like a complete idiot, still kneeling there on the floor.

He rose, too, and reminded himself that he wasn't going to grab her, wasn't going to try to kiss some sense into her. "This is just not going the way I pictured it."

She took his hand. He tried to find some comfort from that, from the fact that she'd touched him, that she looked up at him with soft eyes and a gentle smile. "We don't have to rush into anything." She brought his fingers to her lips and she kissed the backs of his knuckles, one by one.

"Tessa." Her name came out rough with all the emotions he wasn't all that good at dealing with. "We can make it work. Give us a chance."

"I am, Carson." Her voice sounded a little rusty, too. "Definitely."

"I gave up a perfectly wonderful wife for you." Where had that come from? He had no clue.

But she didn't take it badly. On the contrary, she chuckled. "I think you gave up your wife so that you could be free to enjoy all the world has to offer you— including a whole bunch of gorgeous women, serially and probably in groups."

"Very funny." He scowled down at her. "And also wrong. I gave up my marriage for *you*. I just didn't realize it at the time. Everything was and is for you. I wanted to be ready when I finally found you."

"That was kind of twisted—but also just beautiful." She went on tiptoe, offering that mouth he somehow never got enough of kissing. He should have resisted. She'd really pissed him off.

But he couldn't. He lowered his head and kissed her, just a quick one, because he couldn't *not* kiss her. "Marry me," he commanded.

She rose up and kissed him again. Her breath smelled of berries and cinnamon. "I can't. Please try to understand."

He caught her shoulders, fingers digging in—until she winced and he loosened his grip. But he didn't let her go. "What do you need?"

"Need?"

"What do I have to do to get you to say yes?"

Her dark eyes searched his face. "Passion fades, Carson."

"Not mine for you."

"It's too early to know that."

"Not for me. What about for you?" He ran the back of his finger up the silky skin on the side of her neck. She shivered a little. He drank in that unwilling response. "Are you afraid you're going to get tired of me?"

Her gaze never wavered. "No. I'm not. You are…more than I ever bargained for. And in the best of all possible ways."

"Good answer. So then, if you trusted me, if you were sure you could count on me and that I would treat our baby right, *then* would you say yes?"

She didn't even have to think it over. "Yes. I would."

"All right, then. Prepare to learn to trust me."

"Only you could make that sound like a threat."

He caught a curl of her hair and wrapped it slowly around his finger. "I'm going to have to fly back to LA today."

Her eyes went stormy. "But you just got here. And weren't we just talking about working things out? How can we do that if you're in LA?"

"Come with me."

"No, Carson. Right now I need to be here. I can't just run away to your world. Not right now."

He pulled his finger free of that shining coil of coffee-colored hair. "I knew you would say that."

"They why ask?"

"Never hurts to try. I won't be gone long. I need to clear my calendar, take care of a few things that can't wait."

"How long is not long?"

"A couple of days, three at the most."

Tessa kissed him goodbye a few minutes later. It was a very long, deep kiss, and it took all the willpower she possessed not to let that one kiss melt into another.

And another after that.

Not to grab his hand and pull him to the bedroom and have her way with him. Preferably more than once.

But that didn't seem right, somehow. Why it didn't, she wasn't exactly sure. Maybe because he was leaving again so quickly. She could get whiplash; he was here and gone so fast.

Of course, she could have flown back with him. He'd asked her to come.

But that didn't seem right, either.

Nothing seemed right.

As she drove back to the boardinghouse, she kept remembering him dropping to his knees in front of her, replaying all the beautiful things he'd said to her. He'd melted her heart with his words—melted her heart and almost her panties.

But she needed to be careful. She lifted a hand from the steering wheel, pressed it to her flat belly and reminded herself that she had more than just her own heart to consider now. Beautiful words were one thing—and hadn't she heard them all before? Hadn't Miles sworn he would love her forever?

For some men, forever didn't last very long. Carson swore he wasn't like that—or at least not anymore, not when it came to her.

But he had been like that once, with Marianne, hadn't he? Yes, everybody made mistakes and what had happened with Marianne had been several years ago. Some relationships just didn't work out.

Still, she just needed to be careful and not allow Carson to do what he did so very well—sweep her right off her feet and into his waiting arms.

In her room at the boardinghouse, she dug into a couple of small projects she had in the works. When she checked her email, she found one from Jason Velasco. He asked how she was doing—and mentioned that "her" job was still available if by any chance she'd changed her mind. He wrote, *I still have that sketchbook of yours. Do you want it back? Excellent work, by the way.*

At first, she felt a little annoyed. Carson had probably put him up to it.

But then, really, so what if Carson had been behind Jason making contact again?

Tessa realized she could get to like Jason. And professionally, it never hurt to cultivate good contacts. She composed a friendly reply and sent it off before going downstairs.

At lunchtime, she helped out in the kitchen and then moved on to laundry duty. When she came back upstairs, her grandmother called her into the kitchen. Melba plied her with iced tea and lemon bars and asked how "things" were going with her and Carson. Tessa looked into her grandma's loving eyes and almost told her about the baby.

But she was only five weeks pregnant. Who could say what the future might bring? Telling her family about the baby could wait awhile.

"He had to return to LA for a few days."

"But he's coming back?"

"That is the plan, yes."

"Will he be staying here?"

"I don't know. I think he's keeping his suite at Maverick Manor, too."

"I hope he stays here. I like your young man. He's very charming and yet direct. And he's helpful, too. Pitches right in. And it's obvious he's in love with you."

"Oh, Grandma…"

"Not that his being in love with you surprises me. Any man with sense would fall in love with you."

She reached across the table and squeezed Melba's arm. "Love you."

"You be sure to tell him we miss him and he should stay here."

"Of course, I'll tell him you miss him. But as for staying here, I think I'll let him decide that for himself."

"Fine, then. Don't tell him. I'll do it myself."

As it turned out, Melba didn't have to tell him.

That night, he texted Tessa: Back with you Sunday. Staying at the boardinghouse. Because I miss you and I need to be close to you.

Can't wait, she texted back.

So you miss me, too. I knew you would.

My grandmother adores you. I have no idea why.

Give her my love.

Give it to her yourself when you get here on Sunday. How long are you staying?

If no disasters arise here, until the end of the month—or until you agree to come back to Malibu with me.

What to say to that? All possible answers seemed dangerous.

Before she could decide on a response, another text popped up from him.

What are you wearing?

She burst into a loud laugh lying there on her bed before texting back. I did not have sex with you this morning and I am not sexting with you tonight.

Come on, just a hint. I really liked those little satin panties with the peekaboo lace on the sides that you were wearing yesterday.

Perv. They're called boy shorts.

And I like them.

She giggled. And then, out of nowhere, her eyes misted over. She stared at his words on the screen, her throat clutching and her heart filled with longing.

Because she loved him. She really did. Even though it was way too soon, even though she feared it couldn't last and she had the baby to think of, too. The baby needed a mom who made good choices, a mom who didn't just rush into marriage because the father offered—well, okay. Carson had more than offered. He really did seem to want to marry her.

And, well, she wanted to marry him, too.

She loved him. And she desperately wanted everything to work out.

Which was why they needed to take it slow.

Tessa? Where'd you go?

I'm right here.

Everything okay?

I miss you, Carson. You've only been gone since this morning and I miss you so much.

Two more days. I'm there.

She whipped a tissue from the box on the nightstand, dabbed at her eyes and then texted, I'm glad. And I should go.

Wait.

The phone vibrated in her hand with his incoming call. She put it to her ear. "What?"

"I need to say good-night to the baby."

Her poor heart melted all over again. She swiped at her eyes some more. "She doesn't understand words yet."

"Put him on, anyway."

"Hold on a sec. You think it's a boy?"

He answered, "I do," in an intimate tone that set her nerves humming.

"Well, *I* think it's a girl."

He chuckled. "Just put him on."

"Fine. Here you go." She pressed her cell to her stomach and heard Carson say something, though she had no idea what. She put it back to her ear. "Done?"

"For now." His voice was rough and tender. "Good night, Tessa."

She disconnected the call before she could end up bawling on the phone to him, crying out her love, promising him anything he wanted, all of her, forever.

If only he would love her back and never leave her.

And never, ever break her heart.

Chapter Thirteen

Carson boarded the plane for Montana at eight Sunday morning. He picked up a Cadillac SUV in Kalispell and headed for Rust Creek Falls, stopping off at Maverick Manor on the way into town to drop off some things he didn't need right away. At a quarter of noon, he pulled into the boardinghouse parking lot. He grabbed his suitcase and briefcase and went in through the back door, which Melba left unlocked during daylight hours.

The back hall was empty, but he could hear voices from the dining room and knew that Claire and Melba would be in the kitchen preparing lunch, with maybe little Bekka there, too. And since it was Sunday, probably Levi as well. And Tessa would most likely be with them, pitching in. Rather than drag his stuff to the kitchen with him, he raced up the backstairs to leave it in his room.

Tessa's door opened as he strode along the upper hall. She emerged, in old jeans and a wrinkled Drive-By

Truckers T-shirt, her hair piled up in the usual messy knot at the top of her head.

She froze at the sight of him, those eyes that tipped up just right at the corners going wide with surprise. "Hey." Breathless. Eyes shining. The moment was unbelievably sweet.

"Hey." His suitcase and briefcase hit the floor with a matched pair of thuds.

She ran for him. He reached out and caught her as she jumped into his arms, wrapping herself around him the way she liked to do. He buried his face in the crook of her neck, sucked in the wonderful scent of her skin. She whispered, "I missed you."

And then she fisted a hand in his hair, pulled his face up to hers and kissed him.

At that moment, as her mouth crashed into his, he was absolutely certain she would say yes, and soon.

Three days later, he wasn't so sure. She kept saying she wasn't ready yet. She kept telling him she needed more time.

Lots more time.

He didn't have lots more time. And they needed to be together from now on, needed to learn *how* to be together, to build on the chemistry and commonality they already shared. A long-distance relationship wasn't going to cut it.

But he couldn't stay in Rust Creek Falls indefinitely. And she wouldn't come to LA with him. Not, she insisted, until she was sure they were going to be together "in a permanent way." He was all for permanent. And he told her so.

And then she would cycle right back around to how

he couldn't know that. Maybe it wouldn't work out. And where would they be then? Where would their baby be?

He reminded himself he still had time. Till the end of the month, before he had to be back in LA to get serious about the brandy liqueur product launch and handle preparations for the new club opening in San Diego. He told himself that no matter what happened, no matter how long she stalled him, he wasn't giving up. He'd find a way to make it work long-distance, if that was all she would give him. He would stick with her, prove himself true to her.

And somehow, they would end up together.

But he hated that bastard Miles, who had messed her over. That loser had made it way too hard for her to trust again. She doubted her own judgment, and she was scared to death to follow her heart. And that left both of them hanging.

Carson needed to break the damn stalemate they seemed to be caught in. Somehow, he needed to find new ways to convince her that he meant what he promised her: that forever could be theirs—hers, his and the baby's—if only she would reach out and claim it.

On Thursday, he went to the Manor to catch up on some business. While he was there, he called Ryan.

"Heard you were in town again." The lawyer sounded way too pleased with himself. "Can't stay away from a certain hot brunette, can you?"

Carson cut to the chase. "I'm in love with Tessa, and I want to marry her, but she won't say yes."

There was dead silence on the other end of the line. Then, finally, Ryan said, "Didn't I tell you this would happen? It's Rust Creek Falls—am I right? Maybe there's something in the water or—"

"Don't push it, Ryan."

"Aw, come on. Let me gloat at least a little."

"No way." Carson tapped the seal of the bottle that sat on the coffee table in front of him. "However, you do get a bottle of really good Scotch."

Ryan chuckled. "You brought me the Drake Imperial?" At Carson's grunt of affirmation, he crowed, "Now I know you're grateful."

"Yes, I am, as a matter of fact. And didn't you also predict that I would move to Rust Creek Falls?"

"Yes, I did."

"I would move here tomorrow if I could. But I can't."

"I'm speechless."

"You're never speechless. And I need your help again."

"Man, whatever you need, it's yours. I'll do what I can."

"Good. Say I had a reputation for not loving children…"

"Well, given that you've told me any number of times that you're never having children, I would probably have to say that your reputation is richly deserved."

"So, then, how do I change that?"

"You're saying Tessa wants children?"

Carson debated his options: tell Ryan the whole story—or not? He decided to hold back. As of now, the baby was nobody's business but Tessa's and his. "Yeah, Tessa wants children—or at least, she doesn't want to marry a man who doesn't want children."

Ryan made a low, thoughtful sound. "Just so we're clear, you *have* changed your mind about kids, then? You really are willing to be a dad one of these days?"

"That's right, I am." *And a lot sooner than you might think.*

"Love." Ryan's tone was downright reverent. "It's amazing."

"When you're through being awestruck, I'm open to ideas."

"Right. Well, I do have suggestions. Two of them. Number one, buy a place here in Rust Creek Falls. Promise Tessa you'll come here as often as possible, at least a few times a year—and mean it. That should help to reassure her she won't be leaving behind the town she loves."

"That's good. I like it."

"I'll text you the number of a good local Realtor."

"Terrific. But what about how to convince Tessa that I do want children?"

"Well, I think you have to spend some time with children as a way to help you prove to yourself and to her that you really do enjoy them."

Enjoy children. That was asking a lot. He did want the baby, but as for kids in general, well, he mostly wanted nothing to do with them until they were old enough to hold a job and appreciate a good cigar.

He asked, "How exactly am I going to spend a lot of time with kids?"

"Easy. Rust Creek Falls is crawling with babies right now. You know about Jamie Stockton?"

"Who?"

"Jamie Stockton. Recently, his wife gave birth to triplets. She didn't make it."

"You mean his wife died having those babies?"

"Soon after. There were complications, and she didn't pull through."

Carson felt vaguely sick. What if that happened to Tessa?

But it wouldn't. *No freaking way.* He wouldn't allow it.

Ryan asked gingerly, "Carson, you okay?"

"I'm fine, I… My God, the poor guy."

"Yeah. Very tough. And Jamie's a rancher. The man's

not only lost his wife—he's on his own running his ranch with three babies to take care of. With all the babies born lately, Country Kids day care is full."

"But isn't Walker Jones opening a Just Us Kids center here any day now?"

"Just Us Kids opened last Monday. But there's another problem. The cost of professional day care for three infants is through the roof. So several women in town have established a baby chain for the triplets."

"A baby what?"

"Chain. People volunteer to give a hand with the little ones so that Jamie can put in a full day's work on the ranch."

"Wait. Hold on. Are you suggesting I should baby-sit *triplets*?"

"Carson, you have to start somewhere. Might as well jump right in. Let me call Fallon O'Reilly. From what I've heard, she's the one running the baby chain."

After he hung up with Ryan, Carson called the Realtor his friend had recommended. He told her what he was looking for, and she promised to show him some houses the following afternoon.

The next morning, when Carson should have been at the Manor dealing with any number of minor business emergencies that kept cropping up in his absence from Drake headquarters, Carson drove out to Jamie Stockton's ranch instead.

A pretty redhead answered the door. "Carson, right? Ryan said you'd be coming. I'm Fallon O'Reilly, a friend of the Stockton family. I'm pretty much in charge of the baby chain." She held out her hand. Carson took it and gave it a shake. "Come on in."

He stepped over the threshold and followed her down a hallway.

She chattered back at him as she went. "Jamie's out mending fence. But he said to tell you thank you."

"Happy to help." He tried to sound confident. But a baby was crying at the end of the hall. He longed to spin on his heel, race back out the front door and burn rubber getting out of there.

Three hours later, he'd not only changed two loaded diapers; he'd rocked all three blue-eyed Stockton babies, whose names were Jared, Henry and Kate. One by one, they wailed when he held them, their little faces going beet red, tiny noses and rosebud mouths twisting, miniature fists flailing. Even worse, when the one he held started crying, one or both of the other two would get going, as well. Poor Fallon would have to settle them all down.

At least the redhead had sense enough not to leave him alone with the children during the ordeal. She told him not to take all the howling personally. "They'll get used to you. You'll see."

The first couple of hours crawled by. All he wanted was out of there. But at the end, Fallon made him hold the smallest baby, Kate, again. He fed Kate a bottle. She started out bawling, same as before. He rocked her gently and kept his body loose, his face calm. Eventually she seemed to settle a little. Finally, with a heavy sigh, she latched on to the nipple, shut her eyes and got to work on that bottle. He wouldn't go so far as to call her happy to have him holding her, but at least she seemed willing to relax and let it happen.

Carson felt pretty damn good by then. Who said he didn't like babies? He did, damn it. He liked babies—and they could learn to like him.

He could do this. *Piece of cake.*

Before he left, Fallon put him on the schedule. He had nine to noon, Tuesday and Thursday, for the next two weeks. Fallon said that most of the time, he would have another babysitter to help him. With three babies to look after, it worked best to have two sets of ready hands. There would definitely be another sitter working with him next time, on Tuesday. After that, well, they would see.

Carson returned to the Manor for an online meeting and to make a few calls. He ordered a sandwich from room service and ended up working until about two.

When he got back to the boardinghouse, Melba met him in the hallway. "I thought I heard you come in. Claire's baking cookies."

"Chocolate chip?" he asked with enthusiasm, though he already knew. The mouthwatering smells of warm sugar, vanilla and melted chocolate had greeted him when he walked in the back door.

"Come with me." Tessa's grandmother led him to the kitchen, where Claire was just taking another batch from the oven.

Melba put three cookies on a plate and filled a glass with milk for him. "There you go." She patted his back and took the seat next to him.

He bit into a warm cookie. "These are perfect, Claire."

Tessa's sister sent him a smile from her spot at the stove just as Tessa herself appeared in the open doorway. She looked amazing, as always, in shorts and a Save the Whales T-shirt, her hair loose on her shoulders, all wild and curly, her unforgettable face scrubbed clean of makeup.

There was that moment again. Their eyes met and— bam. He'd never met a woman like her. She did something to him, rearranged every molecule in his body with nothing more than a look.

They were going to make it. They would be a family. It was all going to work out.

He wouldn't have it any other way.

She grabbed a plate and chose two cookies for herself, then dropped into the seat next to him. A little groan escaped her as she took that first bite. He did love a woman who ate like she meant it. "Best ever, Claire," she said, then slid him a glance. "How's everything over at Maverick Manor?"

"Fine. I took a long meeting with a group of distributors, made some calls, handled email."

"Sounds productive."

He laid it on her. "And before that I spent three hours at Jamie Stockton's ranch helping Fallon O'Reilly look after Jamie's triplets."

Slowly, Tessa set down the remains of her cookie. Claire and Melba shared a look, and Melba patted him fondly on the back again. Oh, he was getting in good with Melba. And that pleased him no end.

A man needed to get in good with his future wife's grandmother.

Tessa finally forced a laugh. "You're not serious."

"Oh, but I am." He ate another delicious bite of warm cookie. "It was touch and go at first. But I'm getting the hang of it. I joined the baby chain for Tuesday and Thursday morning next week and the week after that."

"Baby chain. By that you mean you're babysitting Jamie Stockton's triplets?" Her tone, hitting midway between stunned and disbelieving, was not especially flattering.

"Yes, I am." He reached for his last cookie.

Tessa stood up and offered her hand. "Come with me."

"As though I could ever refuse you anything." He turned to the others. "Melba, Claire. Thanks for the cookies." The women gave him nods and smiles as he rose and followed Tessa out.

At the base of the back stairs, she turned to him. "What are you up to?" The words made demands, but her tone was sweet. Tender. Maybe even pleased.

He swallowed the last bite of his cookie and brushed the crumbs from his hands. Then he touched her. Because he wanted to. Because she always felt so right. Because he couldn't imagine the rest of his life without her in it. He traced his finger down her soft cheek, guided a wild curl away from her eye. "Finding out if maybe I could like babies."

"And?"

He bent close and brushed a kiss across her lips. "I'm thinking it's doable."

"Carson…" She said it on a cookie-scented sigh, those dark eyes shining up at him.

"I have an idea. I'm thinking we could do it together, take care of Jamie Stockton's triplets. I'll call Fallon and tell her I have another victim—I mean, babysitter."

She smiled at his silly joke, but then she caught her lower lip between her teeth and worried it a little. "Babies always cry when I hold them."

"I understand. Believe me. They do the same with me. Today was two and a half hours of nonstop wailing. I couldn't wait for it to be over. But I stuck with it. And then near the end, the baby girl, Kate, gave in and let me hold her. I fed her a bottle. I have to say, once you get a fresh diaper on them and they finally stop yowling, they're kind of cute."

She gazed up at him so steadily. "Tuesday and Thursday, you said?"

He nodded. "Nine to noon."

"Well, all right. You call Fallon. Tell her I'll be coming with you to help out."

"Excellent. And about this afternoon. You free?"

She went on tiptoe and kissed him. "I am."

"Good. I've got three houses to look at and I want you to come see them with me."

"Houses? Why?"

"Don't ask so many questions. Just be patient. Everything will become crystal clear in the end."

It was after five when they finished touring the last house. A two-story tan clapboard with black shutters, the place was a fixer-upper on five acres just a mile southwest of town, not far from the Crawford ranch, the Shooting Star.

The Realtor shook their hands and said she would call Carson in the morning to talk about the properties they'd seen and to offer a few more houses he might want to look at. He and Tessa stood on the front step and watched her get in her car and drive away.

"Sit with me." He pulled Tessa down beside him on the top step. "So, what do you think?"

"I think you haven't explained to me what is going on."

He entwined his fingers with hers. "I can't move here year-round."

"I know."

"However, I'm actually to the point where I would do it, for you—and also because I somehow feel more at home here than I ever have anywhere else."

She squeezed his fingers. "You feel at home here? Really?"

He met her eyes and never wanted to look away.

"Maybe it's Claire's cooking. Or the way your grandmother treats me like one of the family."

"She's a card-carrying member of the Carson Drake fan club, and that is no lie."

He teased, "You don't have to sound so perplexed about it."

"I'm not. We all know your charms are legendary."

"You noticed. Excellent. Now, where was I? Oh, yeah. I would move here, but I can't run my businesses effectively unless I'm in LA most of the year."

"You really…" Her soft voice broke and the words got lost. But she found them again. "You really mean that? You would do that? Move to Rust Creek Falls?"

"I would if I could, for you. For the baby."

She leaned her head on his shoulder. "It's so crazy. I think I believe you."

He switched hands, taking hers with his right hand, wrapping his left arm around her shoulders. "Maybe someday, when our son is all grown up and ready to take over the Drake companies—"

"Carson," she chided. But he heard the smile in her voice. "She's not even born yet."

"You're right. And I don't want to make his choices for him, anyway. But right now, what I *can* do is buy a house here. I figure I can get away a few times a year, stay a few weeks each visit." She didn't reply, but she did hold his hand a little tighter. He said, "I want you to help me choose the house."

She tipped her head back. Her eyes were stormy, full of longing. And doubt. "I need more time, Carson. Please try to understand. You're being so completely wonderful. I *want* to go for it, marry you, move to LA and be with you. But then I start thinking that I've only known you for a matter of weeks. Yes, we made a baby. And, yes, we need to deal with that. But I don't want to rush into anything. It's too soon. And I refuse to make the same big mistakes all over again."

Don't compare me to that douche bag. Somehow he managed not to say that. He kept his breathing even, held the angry words inside. Instead, he asked her gently, "Did I say the M word just then?"

"No, but—"

"Did I ask you again to move to LA with me?"

"No, you didn't."

"All I said is I'm buying a house here, and it's important to me that you like the house I choose."

Another silence from her. But at least she didn't let go of his hand. Finally, she offered, "Well, if you want my opinion…"

"Please."

"Something on Falls Mountain, maybe? With lots of windows and great views."

He thought of Collin and Willa Traub's house, tucked among the big trees, with the world spread out below them. "I like that idea, though it could be hard to get to in the winter."

"Collin and Willa seem to manage. And as you said, you'll only be here a few times a year. You could easily skip our Montana winters. They can be pretty rough."

He tried not to be annoyed that she assumed he couldn't take the winters, that she spoke so easily of him in the singular, without her. Instead, he drew satisfaction from the knowledge that they'd both been thinking of the Traubs and their gorgeous rustic house. "I have a feeling Christmas in Montana is something I won't want to miss. Christmas on Falls Mountain. I like it. I want that."

She chuckled then. The sound wrapped around his heart. "Well then, you'd better get that Realtor on it—don't you think?"

The next morning, Saturday, when the Realtor called, he told her he wanted property on Falls Mountain. She said she'd check around a little and call him back in an hour.

Fifty minutes later, she called again. "I have one house available. It's just a cabin, really. Six hundred square feet. On the northwest slope."

"Too small."

"Yes. You'd be buying it for the land, and then you would have to build."

"I'd like to see it—and now you've got me wondering. How about any other nice pieces of property on the mountain? Just the land, I mean. I could build my own place. Anything available?"

"You've read my mind, Carson. I have two parcels you can look at. One is halfway up, not far from the falls. The other's nearer the summit."

He told her he wanted to see all three—the cabin and the two parcels. She said she could show them to him that day, and he agreed to meet her at the cabin at one o'clock.

When he hung up, he tapped on Tessa's door. A moment later, it swung open. She had a pencil stuck behind her ear and a curl falling over her eye. She blew the curl aside.

He resisted the need to get his hands on her. Bracing an arm on the door frame, he asked, "Working?"

"Catching up on a few things, yeah."

"How about a ride up Falls Mountain?"

Her slow smile lit a fire down in the core of him.

"The Realtor found some possibilities?" At his nod, she asked, "When?"

"We should leave in the next twenty minutes or so."

"I'm in."

He couldn't bear not touching her, after all. So he reached out and guided that misbehaving curl away from her eye and behind the ear without the pencil in it. Her skin was cool satin. "Can you swim at the falls?"

"Yes, though it's really cold. There's a pool at the base."

"Do I need a suit?" Skinny-dipping held definite appeal.

"Sorry, but yeah. On a pretty Saturday in July, the odds are high we won't be alone."

"Board shorts, it is. And let's take a picnic. After we're done seeing properties, we can visit the falls. Swim. Have some lunch."

"Twenty minutes. I'll meet you in the kitchen, and I'll have our lunch ready." Before he could steal a kiss, she shut the door on him.

They saw the cabin property first. It was deep in the woods, on the north side of the mountain where the sunlight was sparse, with no views to speak of.

Tessa shook her head. "This isn't the one."

He agreed with her.

Next they drove to the land near the summit.

"This is more like it," he said as they stood on a point overlooking the rolling valley below. He would build the house back toward the hillside, with lots of wide windows facing the view, and he'd get with Collin, make a plan to pave the road that turned to dirt on the second half of the ride up here.

Because he *would* be coming to Rust Creek Falls every

Christmas. And Tessa and their baby would be coming with him.

Tessa said, "I'm guessing this is it." She gave him a look—full of excitement and pleasure.

It took all the will he had not to drop to his knees in the dirt right then and there, in front of God and the Realtor and all those tall trees, not to beg her all over again to wear his ring. Somehow he kept hold of himself.

They got in the vehicles and drove down to the land near the falls. It was a nice piece of property, but it didn't compare with the one higher up.

He told the Realtor that he would meet her Sunday afternoon at her office to make an offer on the property near the summit. She said she would call the owner's Realtor and let him know the offer was on the way. Then, with a last wave, she got in her mini-SUV and headed down the mountain.

It wasn't far to the falls. They found a parking spot by the road and took a little trail that wound among the bracken toward the roar of the falling water.

In no time, the trail opened up to a flat section of bank and the falls high above. It was a gorgeous sight, the wall of water spinning and foaming as it fell, droplets gleaming like diamonds in the shafts of sunlight that found their way through the trees as the water tumbled into the pool below.

Best of all, they were alone. No one else had decided to visit the falls that afternoon—at least not so far.

He spread a blanket on the bank, and she set down the picnic basket and their towels. They stripped off boots and socks, jeans and shirts. He got down to board shorts. And just the sight of her standing there in a red-and-white polka-dot bikini reminded him forcefully of how much he wanted her.

"Last one in's a city girl!" he taunted and ran for the pool.

"Cheater!" she shouted and took off after him.

He got there first and ran right in, with her close on his heels.

"It's freezing!" He dunked himself, fast, just to get it over with.

"Told you so." She laughed and started splashing him.

"Now you're going to get it." He jumped on her and dunked her. She shot out of the water a moment later, droplets flying every which way as she shook her head from side to side.

"You drive me crazy." He grabbed for her, needing to pull her close and steal a long, hot kiss in the icy, churning water.

But she shoved him away with a teasing laugh and swam for the falls. He chased after her. She swam fast, vanishing under the falling water, with him close on her heels.

It was eerie and gorgeous behind the falls, the echo of the tumbling water a constant, slightly muted roar, rough gray rock rising up around them on three sides. She swam to the curve of the cliff face and held out a hand for him.

He took it. She pulled him toward her.

As soon as he found his balance on the rock, he reeled her in. Laughing, she let him hold her.

He kissed her then, finally. Her lips were cold, her body covered in chill bumps.

"I could kiss you forever," he said, when they finally came up for air. "Tessa. I love you." *There*. He had said it outright. The world seemed to stop on its axis as they stared at each other. "I swear to you. You're the only woman for me."

She gazed up at him, her lips slightly parted. And then she whispered so sweetly, "And I love you."

It was a great moment. He wanted to wrap it in tissue paper, tie it with a satin bow, save it in his heart and soul for all time. *Marry me*, he almost demanded.

But she must have known what he would say, must have seen it in his eyes. She touched her cold fingers to his mouth. "Don't…"

And he let her stop him. He pressed his lips together over the words, held back the demands that tried to push from his throat. He knew in his head that it hadn't been all that long since the Memorial Day Baby Bonanza Parade, when he first caught sight of her in that silly stork costume and knew he had to meet her. A matter of weeks, that was all. A month and a half.

But he also knew what he wanted. And she'd just said she loved him. They needed to get started on their life together. It hurt him, killed him a little, every time she told him no.

"Carson," she coaxed, her voice warm and tender, though the icy water pebbled her skin and she shivered in his hold. She curled her cold little hand around the nape of his neck and pulled him down for another kiss. "I love you," she whispered.

He drank those words from her parted lips, wrapping her tighter, kissing her endlessly.

Finally, she pulled away and admitted, "My teeth are chattering. Let's go back to the blanket and dry off before I freeze to death."

Reluctantly, he released her and followed her back through the veil of tumbling water. They swam to the bank, climbed out and ran for the blanket. She was still shivering, so he pulled her between his legs, grabbed her towel and rubbed her hair and then her shoulders.

He couldn't resist kissing her. Something about her just drove him wild. He pressed his lips to her still-wet hair, licked the water off her cold cheek, kissed his way downward to the crook of her neck, where he nipped her with his teeth.

She laughed, twisting in his hold to face him as she teasingly batted him away. "Stop that. Don't you—" She stiffened in his arms, her eyes locked on something over his left shoulder.

He searched her suddenly pale face. "What?"

"Look." She said it way too softly, staring wide-eyed at whatever it was behind him.

Stark alarm hollowing his gut, he turned his head and looked.

Slowly, crouching low, a full-grown mountain lion emerged from the rim of trees that surrounded the pool. Its black eyes pinned them. The laid-back ears and long, twitching tail said it all. The cat had identified them as prey.

For Carson, time stalled.

The roar of the falls receded beneath the roaring of his own blood in his ears. His heart pounded hard and deep, every nerve rising to high alert, each muscle drawing tight.

He knew total fear. It was invigorating. Everything came crystal clear.

An image of his late father flashed in his head. Beyond how to use a rifle and track big game, Declan Drake had taught Carson the habits of all the larger predators.

As a rule, mountain lions were solitary creatures, shy of man. But if they got really hungry or were ill or injured, all bets were off.

This cat had blood on its flank. It had been wounded

and now all its instincts pushed it to retaliate, to attack. Somehow, Carson was going to have to take it down.

"Go," he said softly to the woman in his arms. Keeping his eyes locked on the lion, he took her shoulders and pushed her up and away. "Don't run. They try to latch on at the back of your neck, so turn and face him. Back away slowly."

He felt her leave him, felt the lack of her as she scrambled up and stumbled back. *Good girl.*

In slow motion, or so it seemed to him, while still on the ground, he turned his body so he fully faced the threat. His mind went blank as adrenaline spurted, and his body reacted automatically, even with his brain on hold. When the world came clear again, he was standing fully upright.

The cat kept coming in absolute silence, moving faster now.

Carson planted his feet wide and spread his arms, trying to look larger, more threatening, trying to change the cat's mind about defining him as prey. He let out a deep, loud bellow of rage for good measure.

Didn't work. The cat never hesitated. It came on faster still.

Carson bellowed again and braced for the fight.

With a feral cry, the lion pounced. Powerful rear legs launching, deadly claws reaching out, it flew straight at him.

Carson punched his right arm forward, ready for the catch.

Chapter Fourteen

Tessa swallowed a scream as the big cat pounced.

She needed a weapon. She needed to help. Sheer terror coursed through her, every nerve on red alert. Instinct ordered her to flee. But her heart was having none of that.

A weapon, damn it! She glanced around frantically.

A big rock, maybe. She didn't see one. *And where is a nice, sturdy stick when you need it?*

Close to hand, she had only a pile of their clothing. She could throw a shoe at the animal, but that wouldn't do much. There was the picnic basket…

Okay, then. She dipped to her knees and scooped it up by the handle.

When she looked again at Carson and the cat, she couldn't believe her eyes. He had the animal by the throat—his long, powerful right arm outstretched. The cat danced on its hind legs, lurching as it struggled. It had its paws wrapped around his arm, sharp claws digging in.

Carson was strangling it. And there was blood. *Carson's blood*. Flowing down his arm, the side of his neck, his shoulder...

"Tessa, get out of here!" he shouted at her.

Her mind went dead blank. What was the matter with her? She needed to stay focused.

And, no, she was not leaving. Forget about that. And the basket? What good was the basket? If she beat the cat with it, maybe. But the goal was to help Carson. She mustn't do anything that would dislodge the stranglehold he had on the animal. Clubbing the cat might jar Carson's grip.

And then she remembered the cheese and salami she'd brought for their lunch. And the knife to cut them with. It wasn't much. But if she could get in close, maybe...

The cat made weird growling, shrieking sounds, gurgling as it struggled. Carson held on. But for how long?

She upended the basket. Cheese and salami, baggies full of summer fruit, and rolls of crackers fell out—and there! *The knife!*

She pounced on it, grabbed it and moved in on the man and the cat.

"No!" Carson shouted. "Tessa, get away! Don't!"

She ignored him, sidling closer, thinking that she had to do something. She raised the knife high.

And in the split second before she brought the knife down, a loud crack sounded.

The cat made the strangest sighing noise—and went limp in Carson's grip.

Tessa let her hand fall. The knife tumbled, forgotten, to the ground. Carson stood so very still, his grip remaining firm around the throat of the cat. Slowly, he lowered the animal to the dirt and gently laid it down.

She ran to him, dropping to a crouch at his side. "Carson..."

"I'm okay."

But he didn't look okay. There was way too much blood. More than one of the gouges on his arm would need stitches.

They both heard the footsteps at the same time and looked up from the still body of the cat to the rim of tall trees. Collin Traub, Nate Crawford, Sheriff Gage Christensen and three other local men emerged into the sunlight. Each carried a rifle.

"Damn good shooting," Carson said in a flat voice.

Sheriff Christensen patted one of the other men on the shoulder. "Tim here's the best there is." He turned his gaze to the cat. "It attacked old Mrs. Calloway's dog up on Eagle Ridge. She shot it. We've been tracking the poor thing to finish it."

Tessa didn't care about any of that. Not right now. "Help me get Carson in the SUV and down to the clinic. He needs a doctor *now*."

Carson walked to the SUV on his own steam. Tessa sent a little prayer of thanks to God that it wasn't that far. Collin offered to drive. It was a steep road with lots of switchbacks, a road that Collin knew well.

Tessa surrendered the wheel and sat in back with Carson, who had her T-shirt and his wrapped around the worst of his injuries. The adrenaline rush was wearing off by then. He was starting to feel the pain, lines etching in his forehead, a rim of white around his beautiful mouth.

He leaned his head on her shoulder. She eased an arm around him and willed Collin to drive faster.

At the clinic, Emmet went right to work. There were shots to numb the pain, a thorough cleaning of each wound—and a lot of stitching. Carson was up-to-date on his tetanus shots. Though the cat had shown no signs of being rabid, Emmet followed protocol and gave Carson the first in a series of rabies shots and also a shot of rabies immune globulin.

Tessa stood by Carson's side, holding his left hand—that arm was uninjured—as he endured Emmet's care. Carson seemed pretty stoic about it, though she didn't see how he could stay so calm. With every prick of the needle, every swipe of sterilized gauze as Emmet cleaned him up, every last stitch as Emmet sewed the wounds shut, Tessa had to keep an iron grip on herself or she would have screamed terrible things at poor Emmet, would have demanded he go easier, be gentler, even though her own eyes told her he was careful, skilled and kind.

She just couldn't bear it, seeing Carson hurt. She tried to take comfort from the fact that he didn't need to be air-lifted to the hospital in Kalispell, that he was conscious through all of it and he didn't even require a transfusion. He had saved them, plain and simple, and he was going to be all right. All that was good, she reminded herself. Much better than it might have been.

Carson would have scars from this. Emmet teased that scars were sexy. Carson actually chuckled at that and shook his head.

The best part was that she got to take him home to the boardinghouse as soon as Emmet was through stitching him up.

As they were leaving, Emmet thanked her for the ads she'd placed back in June. More medical help was on the way. And Rust Creek Falls needed it. In the past week, there had been a sudden spike in pediatric illnesses. With all the new babies in town, the clinic was really having trouble providing needed services.

Tessa gave Emmet a quick hug and whispered, "Thank *you*, for taking such good care of Carson."

Someone must have called her grandmother because Melba and Gene were waiting in the boardinghouse parking lot when they drove in. Melba hustled them inside and said she had a bed ready in a downstairs room if Carson couldn't manage the stairs.

He put his good arm around her. "It's okay, Melba, really. I can make it up to my room."

Her grandmother stared up at him with tears in her eyes. "It was such a brave thing you did."

He glanced at Tessa. She felt that quick look as a physical caress. "In a situation like that, a man just does what he has to do."

Melba said, "I praise the Lord you're going to be okay."

He kissed her on the forehead. "I am fine—I promise."

"No, you're not," she argued tartly. "But you will be. And that's what matters."

"Come on, son," said Old Gene. "Let's get you upstairs."

In his room, Melba fussed over him terribly. Tessa shooed her grandmother and grandfather out to the hallway and helped him into a pair of sweats and a clean T-shirt.

When Melba bustled back in, Tessa ducked into her own room to get out of her still-damp bikini and into dry clothes.

When she went back to the room next door, Melba was getting him comfortable, arranging his pillows just so. He admitted that, yes, he was hungry, so Claire brought up lunch for him and served him right there in bed. Levi brought Bekka in, to see for herself that "Car-Car," as Bekka called him, was going to be all right.

Finally, almost an hour after they pulled into the parking lot, Tessa's family left them alone.

Carson patted the bed on his good side. Tessa couldn't get there fast enough. She crawled in beside him and cuddled close, pressing a kiss to the side of his throat that didn't have a bandage on it.

"I love you," she whispered in his ear. She had a whole bunch more to say—so much. Everything that mattered.

But he only gathered her closer, pressed his lips to her hair and let out a slow sigh.

When she tipped her head back to look at him, his eyes were shut. She watched as his breathing evened out and he slept.

Tessa drifted off, too.

When she woke a couple of hours later, he was lying on his good side, watching her.

She hid a yawn. "Do you need one of those pain pills Emmet gave you?"

He shook his head. "I was just trying to figure a few things out, trying to work out how to tell you…"

"What?"

"First, what you did was dangerous, stepping in with that knife when I told you to get away."

She almost laughed but somehow held it in. "Are you going to lecture me for not running off and leaving you there?"

"Yeah." His voice was rough with emotion. "You could have been hurt, and you put yourself in danger. And I can't stand to think that maybe—"

"So don't think it. And spare us both the lecture. It's not going to do any good. You needed help, and I was bound to give it. That's what people do when there's trouble—especially when there's trouble for someone they love."

"If something had happened to you—"

She stopped him with a kiss. "It didn't. Let it go."

A little grunt of pain escaped him as he shifted. "I did have it handled."

"I saw that. But it was taking too long, and you were hurt. And I just…needed to speed things up."

"With your trusty cheese knife."

They stared at each other. And then they both started laughing. It felt so good, to lie there with him, sharing silly and slightly hysterical laughter, safe and cozy together in her grandmother's house.

Finally, he said, "I'm definitely going to need an extra arm to take care of Jamie Stockton's triplets on Tuesday."

"Use mine."

Dark eyes gleamed. "I was hoping you'd say that. Thank you. I will. Here's a question for you. How am I going to bear it in a couple of weeks when I have to leave you?"

She gazed at him steadily, sure in her heart, in every part of herself, at last. "You're not."

He reached out with his bad arm, wincing as he moved it. And he traced her eyebrows, one and then the other, his touch featherlight. "How so?"

She put it right out there. "Because you're going to take me with you."

His eyes widened, warmed, even misted over a little. "Damn. Do you really mean that?"

With a laugh of pure joy, she slid back off the bed.

"Hey!" He tried to reach for her, but his injuries slowed him down a bit. "Get back up here." She shook her head as she went over the edge to the floor. "Tessa, what are you doing?"

She came up on her knees and stretched out her hand

to him. He took it with his right hand, grunting in pain as he moved his bad arm. "Oops. Sorry." She tried to let go.

But he held on. "Too late. I've got you now. What's going on?"

And she did it. She said it. It was all so very simple. "Carson, I love you. I want to spend my life with you. I want to be there, if you're ever in danger, if you're ever alone and need someone to lean on. I've been so worried that I couldn't count on you. But now I see that I couldn't bear it if you needed me and I wasn't there for *you* to count on. I have to be there for you, Carson. I need to be at your side. I just…well, I guess there's something about a life-and-death situation that brings everything so very clear."

He stared at her intently, as though he would never look away. "I noticed that, yes."

"I'm not afraid anymore, Carson. You're nothing like any man I've ever known before. What happened in the past, the bad choices and stupid mistakes that I made— I own them. I learned from them. I'm ready to move on. Ready for *you*, Carson. Because with you, it's so different. With you, it's so good. I love you and I trust you and I want to be with you. I want to marry you and move to California with you. I want to build a house with you up on Falls Mountain where we can come when we want to get away. I want you with me when our baby is born. I want us to raise her together. I want us, you and me, to be together in the deepest way, as husband and wife. I want it all with you, Carson. Please make me the happiest woman in the world. Please say that you'll marry me and be my husband for all of our lives."

"Yes." His voice rumbled up, thick with love and hope and longing. "Dear God, how I love you." He tugged on her hand. "Damn it, Tessa. Why are you on the floor?"

"I'm on my knees. You know, like people do when they propose?"

"Get up here."

She didn't have to be told twice. She surged up.

And then he said, "Wait." She just stood there by the bed, feeling slightly bewildered. "The bureau. Top left-hand drawer. Front right corner." She blinked at him, confused.

He chuckled. "Go. Open the drawer. Look."

So she went over there, opened the drawer, pushed his T-shirts aside and found the red leather ring box trimmed in gold. "Oh, Carson…"

"Your grandmother told me your size." His voice was as ragged and rough as her own. "I hope it's okay."

She flipped the top back, saw the giant diamond and the matching platinum band. "Oh, Carson, it's beautiful."

"You're sure? Because if you want, we can—"

"It's perfect." She took out the engagement ring and put the box with the wedding band still in it back in the drawer. Then she gave the diamond to him and held down her hand. He slipped it on her finger. It glittered so brightly. Tears filled her eyes. "Just exactly right."

"Come here," he commanded.

She didn't have to be told twice. She joined him on the bed, and he pulled her into the shelter of his good arm.

When his lips met hers, it was a promise. *Their* promise. For now and forever.

For the rest of their lives.

Epilogue

They were married two weeks later, out in the national forest, in a high meadow with the Rocky Mountains all around them.

Tessa wore a strapless white dress with a poufy white skirt and a vivid red satin sash. Her bouquet was all roses—red, white and blue. She wanted a patriotic wedding and she got one. In honor of Memorial Day, the day that they met.

After the ceremony, they went down into town for a red, white and blue reception in Rust Creek Falls Park. There was barbecue and wedding punch. The guests took turns guarding the punch bowl to keep Homer Gilmore from getting up to his old tricks.

Homer did put in an appearance to wish the bride and groom a lifetime of happiness—and to offer Carson one more chance at the magic moonshine. Carson thanked him for the good wishes, told him again that the deal was off and warned him to stay away from the punch bowl.

The cake was five layers, decked out in Old Glory colors, flags flying over the bride-and-groom topper. And after dark, as Tessa and Carson danced beneath the moon, Melba, Gene, Tessa's mom and dad and her two sisters passed out wedding sparklers. Willa Traub, Callie Crawford, Kristen and Ryan Roarke and several other friends hurried to get them all lit. Tessa whirled in her new husband's arms as the sparklers flashed and glittered all around them, bright and golden, lighting up the night.

Ten months after their wedding, on Memorial Day, Tessa woke in their new vacation house on Falls Mountain to the sound of a baby crying. Another cry joined the first.

The twins, Declan and Charlotte, were awake.

Tessa cuddled closer to Carson, wrapping her leg across his lean waist, pressing her lips to the hard curve of his shoulder.

He kissed the top of her head and grumbled, "I know. It's my turn." He sat up and swung his legs off the far side of the bed.

She stretched and yawned. "I'll get the coffee going for you."

Not much later, he brought the babies into the great room. Tessa sat in the big rocker, and he helped her get settled to nurse them in tandem.

It was a challenge, taking care of twins. But Tessa had found she loved every minute of being Charlotte and Declan's mom. As it turned out, once she put her mind and heart into it, she wasn't such a disaster with babies, after all.

And about that job with IMI? She'd changed her mind and taken it. A month after the wedding, she'd gone to work for Jason Velasco. IMI was a progressive company.

They gave her a flexible schedule with a lot of time working from home. Plus, she'd chosen an excellent, loving nanny, so the babies were happy when she and Carson had to work. True, pumping milk for twins at her desk was getting old fast. But so far, she was managing.

Charlotte finished breakfast first. Carson took her off to change her diaper. Once Declan was done, Tessa changed him, too, and then carried him back to the great room. She laid him down beside his sister on the play mat in front of the big window that looked out over the Rust Creek Valley, green and glorious far below in the light of the rising sun. She set the mobiles spinning, and the babies seemed happy enough for that moment to lie there and watch them.

Carson held down a hand to her. She took it, and he pulled her up into his waiting arms. He kissed her long and slow. "It's our anniversary, remember?"

"How could I ever forget?"

"A year to the day since I first saw you at the Memorial Day Baby Bonanza Parade."

"With my dorky yellow beak and my big orange feet."

He laughed, and then he kissed her again. When he lifted his head, he tipped her chin up with a finger. "You changed my life. I thought I was doing just fine before you came along. I thought I was happy. I didn't know what happiness was."

"I love you." Her voice was husky with emotion. "Always." She rested her hand on his right arm, traced the ridges of scar tissue under her fingers, loving the feel of them. They were a keepsake, a reminder of all they had together, of all they held precious. Of what they could have lost. "So?" she asked. "Breakfast?"

He nodded. "And then we'll take the twins down into town for the parade."

"And to the barbecue in the park after that."

"And then to the boardinghouse to say hi to Great-Grandma Melba."

She beamed up at him. "It's going to be a beautiful day."

* * * * *

Don't miss the next installment of
the new Special Edition continuity
MONTANA MAVERICKS: THE BABY BONANZA
Cowboy doctor Jonathan Clifton isn't looking to put
down roots or let anyone get too close to him.
Until he meets clinic nurse Dawn Laramie, that is!
Can this be love at last?

Look for
HER MAVERICK MD
by Teresa Southwick
On sale August 2016, wherever
Harlequin books and ebooks are sold.

*Officer Wyn Bailey has found herself wanting
more from her boss—and older brother's best friend—
for a while now. Will sexy police chief Cade Emmett
let his guard down long enough to embrace
the love he secretly craves?*

*Read on for a sneak peek at the newest book
in* New York Times *bestselling author
RaeAnne Thayne's* HAVEN POINT *series,
RIVERBEND ROAD,
available July 2016 from HQN Books.*

CHAPTER ONE

"THIS WAS YOUR dire emergency? Seriously?"

Officer Wynona Bailey leaned against her Haven Point Police Department squad car, not sure whether to laugh or pull out her hair. "That frantic phone call made it sound like you were at death's door!" she exclaimed to her great-aunt Jenny. "You mean to tell me I drove here with full lights and sirens, afraid I would stumble over you bleeding on the ground, only to find you in a stand-off with a baby moose?"

The gangly-looking creature had planted himself in the middle of the driveway while he browsed from the shrubbery that bordered it. He paused in his chewing to watch the two of them out of long-lashed dark eyes.

He was actually really cute, with big ears and a curious face. She thought about pulling out her phone to take a picture that her sister could hang on the local wildlife bulletin board in her classroom but decided Jenny probably wouldn't appreciate it.

"It's not the calf I'm worried about," her great-aunt said. "It's his mama over there."

She followed her aunt's gaze and saw a female moose on the other side of the willow shrubs, watching them with much more caution than her baby was showing.

While the creature might look docile on the outside, Wyn knew from experience a thousand-pound cow could move at thirty-five miles an hour and wouldn't hesitate to take on anything she perceived as a threat to her offspring.

"I need to get into my garage, that's all," Jenny practically wailed. "If Baby Bullwinkle there would just move two feet onto the lawn, I could squeeze around him, but he won't budge for anything."

She had to ask the logical question. "Did you try honking your horn?"

Aunt Jenny glared at her, looking as fierce and stern as she used to when Wynona was late turning in an assignment in her aunt's high school history class.

"Of course I tried honking my horn! And hollering at the stupid thing and even driving right up to him, as close as I could get, which only made the mama come over to investigate. I had to back up again."

Wyn's blood ran cold, imagining the scene. That big cow could easily charge the sporty little convertible her diminutive great-aunt had bought herself on her seventy-fifth birthday.

What would make them move along? Wynona sighed, not quite sure what trick might disperse a couple of stubborn moose. Sure, she was trained in Krav Maga martial arts, but somehow none of those lessons seemed to apply in this situation.

The pair hadn't budged when she pulled up with her lights and sirens blaring in answer to her aunt's desperate phone call. Even if she could get them to move, scaring them out of Aunt Jenny's driveway would probably only migrate the problem to the neighbor's yard.

She was going to have to call in backup from the state wildlife division.

"Oh, no!" her aunt suddenly wailed. "He's starting on the honeysuckle! He's going to ruin it. Stop! Move it. Go on now." Jenny started to climb out of her car again, raising and lowering her arms like a football referee calling a touchdown.

"Aunt Jenny, get back inside your vehicle!" Wyn exclaimed.

"But the honeysuckle! Your dad planted that for me the summer before he...well, you know."

Wyn's heart gave a sharp little spasm. Yes. She *did* know. She pictured the sturdy, robust man who had once watched over his aunt, along with everybody else in town. He wouldn't have hesitated for a second here, would have known exactly how to handle the situation.

Wynnie, anytime you're up against something bigger than you, just stare 'em down. More often than not, that will do the trick.

Some days, she almost felt like he was riding shotgun next to her.

"Stay in your car, Jenny," she said again. "Just wait there while I call Idaho Fish and Game to handle things. They probably need to move them to higher ground."

"I don't have time to wait for some yahoo to load up his tranq gun and hitch up his horse trailer, then drive over from Shelter Springs! Besides that honeysuckle, which is priceless to me, I have seventy-eight dollars' worth of groceries in the trunk of my car that will be ruined if I can't get into the house. That includes four pints of Ben & Jerry's Cherry Garcia that's going to be melted red goo if I don't get it in the freezer fast—and that stuff is not exactly cheap, you know."

Her great-aunt looked at her with every expectation that she would fix the problem and Wyn sighed again. Small-town police work was mostly about problem solving—and when she happened to have been born and raised in that small town, too many people treated her like their own private security force.

"I get it. But I'm calling Fish and Game."

"You've got a piece. Can't you just fire it into the air or something?"

Yeah, unfortunately, her great-aunt—like everybody else in town—watched far too many cop dramas on TV and thought that was how things were done.

"Give me two minutes to call Fish and Game, then I'll see if I can get him to move aside enough that you can pull into your driveway. Wait in your car," she ordered for the fourth time as she kept an eye on Mama Moose. "Do not, I repeat, do *not* get out again. Promise?"

Aunt Jenny slumped back into her seat, clearly disappointed that she wasn't going to have front row seats to some kind of moose-cop shoot-out. "I suppose."

To Wyn's relief, local game warden Moose Porter—who, as far as she knew, was no relation to the current troublemakers—picked up on the first ring. She explained the situation to him and gave him the address.

"You're in luck. We just got back from relocating a female brown bear and her cub away from that campground on Dry Creek Road. I've still got the trailer hitched up."

"Thanks. I owe you."

"How about that dinner we've been talking about?" he asked.

She had not been talking about dinner. Moose had been pretty relentless in asking her out for months and she always managed to deflect. It wasn't that she didn't like the guy. He was nice and funny and good-looking in a burly, outdoorsy, flannel-shirt-and-gun-rack sort of way, but she didn't feel so much as an ember around him. Not like, well, someone else she preferred not to think about.

Maybe she would stop thinking about that *someone else* if she ever bothered to go on a date. "Sure," she said on impulse. "I'm pretty busy until after Lake Haven Days, but let's plan something in a couple of weeks. Meantime, how soon can you be here?"

"Great! I'll definitely call you. And I've got an ETA of about seven minutes now."

The obvious delight left her squirming and wishing she had deflected his invitation again.

Fish or cut line, her father would have said.

"Make it five, if you can. My great-aunt's favorite honeysuckle bush is in peril here."

"On it."

She ended the phone call just as Jenny groaned, "Oh. Not the butterfly bush, too! Shoo. Go on, move!"

While she was on the phone, the cow had moved around the shrubs nearer her calf and was nibbling on the large showy blossoms on the other side of the driveway.

Wyn thought about waiting for the game warden to handle the situation, but Jenny was counting on her. She couldn't let a couple of moose get the better of her. Wondering idly if a Kevlar vest would protect her in the event she was charged, she climbed out of her patrol vehicle and edged around to the front bumper. "Come on. Move along. That's it."

She opted to move toward the calf, figuring the cow would follow her baby. Mindful to keep the vehicle between her and the bigger animal, she waved her arms like she was directing traffic in a big-city intersection. "Go. Get out of here."

Something in her firm tone or maybe her rapid-fire movements finally must have convinced the calf she wasn't messing around this time. He paused for just a second, then lurched through a break in the shrubs to the other side, leaving just enough room for Great-Aunt

Jenny to squeeze past and head for her garage to unload
her groceries.

"Thank you, Wynnie. You're the best," her aunt called.
"Come by one of these Sundays for dinner. I'll make my
fried chicken and biscuits and my Better-Than-Sex cake."

Her mouth watered and her stomach rumbled, reminding her quite forcefully that she hadn't eaten anything
since her shift started that morning.

Her great-aunt's Sunday dinners were pure decadence.
Wyn could almost feel her arteries clog in anticipation.

"I'll check my schedule."

"Thanks again."

Jenny drove her flashy little convertible into the garage and quickly closed the door behind her.

Of all things, the sudden action of the door seemed
to startle the big cow moose where all other efforts—
including a honking horn and Wyn's yelling and arm-
peddling—had failed. The moose shied away from the
activity, heading in Wyn's direction.

Crap.

Heart pounding, she managed to jump into her vehicle
and yank the door closed behind her seconds before the
moose charged past her toward the calf.

The two big animals picked their way across the lawn
and settled in to nibble Jenny's pretty red-twig dogwoods.

Crisis managed—or at least her part in it—she turned
around and drove back to the street just as a pickup pulling a trailer with the Idaho Fish and Game logo came into
view over the hill.

She pushed the button to roll down her window and
Moose did the same. Beside him sat a game warden she
didn't know. Moose beamed at her and she squirmed,
wishing she had shut him down again instead of giving
him unrealistic expectations.

"It's a cow and her calf," she said, forcing her tone into a brisk, businesslike one and addressing both men in the vehicle. "They're now on the south side of the house."

"Thanks for running recon for us," Moose said.

"Yeah. Pretty sure we managed to save the Ben & Jerry's, so I guess my work here is done."

The warden grinned at her and she waved and pulled onto the road, leaving her window down for the sweet-smelling June breezes to float in.

She couldn't really blame a couple of moose for wandering into town for a bit of lunch. This was a beautiful time around Lake Haven, when the wildflowers were starting to bloom and the grasses were long and lush.

She loved Haven Point with all her heart, but she found it pretty sad that the near-moose encounter was the most exciting thing that had happened to her on the job in days.

Her cell phone rang just as she turned from Clover Hill Road to Lakeside Drive. She knew by the ringtone just who was on the other end and her breathing hitched a little, like always. Those stone-cold embers she had been wondering about when it came to Moose Porter suddenly flared to thick, crackling life.

Yeah. She knew at least one reason why she didn't go out much.

She pushed the phone button on her vehicle's hands-free unit. "Hey, Chief."

"Hear you had a little excitement this afternoon and almost tangled with a couple of moose."

She heard the amusement in the voice of her boss—and friend—and tried not to picture Cade Emmett stretched out behind his desk, big and rangy and gorgeous, with that surprisingly sweet smile that broke hearts all over Lake Haven County.

"News travels."

"Your great-aunt Jenny just called to inform me you risked your life to save her Cherry Garcia and to tell me all about how you deserve a special commendation."

"If she really thought that, why didn't she at least give me a pint for my trouble?" she grumbled.

The police chief laughed, that rich, full laugh that made her fingers and toes tingle like she'd just run full tilt down Clover Hill Road with her arms outspread.

Curse the man.

"You'll have to take that up with her next time you see her. Meantime, we just got a call about possible trespassers at that old wreck of a barn on Darwin Twitchell's horse property on Conifer Drive, just before the turnoff for Riverbend. Would you mind checking it out before you head back for the shift change?"

"Who called it in?"

"Darwin. Apparently somebody tripped an alarm he set up after he got hit by our friendly local graffiti artist a few weeks back."

Leave it to the ornery old buzzard to set a trap for unsuspecting trespassers. Knowing Darwin and his contrariness, he probably installed infrared sweepers and body heat sensors, even though the ramshackle barn held absolutely nothing of value.

"The way my luck is going today, it's probably a relative to the two moose I just made friends with."

"It could be a skunk, for all I know. But Darwin made me swear I'd send an officer to check it out. Since the graffiti case is yours, I figured you'd want first dibs, just in case you have the chance to catch them red-handed. Literally."

"Gosh, thanks."

He chuckled again and the warmth of it seemed to

ease through the car even through the hollow, tinny Bluetooth speakers.

"Keep me posted."

"Ten-four."

She turned her vehicle around and headed in the general direction of her own little stone house on Riverbend Road that used to belong to her grandparents.

The Redemption mountain range towered across the lake, huge and imposing. The snow that would linger in the moraines and ridges above the timberline for at least another month gleamed in the afternoon sunlight and the lake was that pure, vivid turquoise usually seen only in shallow Caribbean waters.

Her job as one of six full-time officers in the Haven Point Police Department might not always be overflowing with excitement, but she couldn't deny that her workplace surroundings were pretty gorgeous.

She spotted the first tendrils of black smoke above the treetops as she turned onto the rutted lane that wound its way through pale aspen trunks and thick pines and spruce.

Probably just a nearby farmer burning some weeds along a ditch line, she told herself, or trying to get rid of the bushy-topped invasive phragmites reeds that could encroach into any marshy areas and choke out all the native species. But something about the black curl of smoke hinted at a situation beyond a controlled burn.

Her stomach fluttered with nerves. She hated fire calls even more than the dreaded DD—domestic disturbance. At least in a domestic situation, there was some chance she could defuse the conflict. Fire was avaricious and relentless, smoke and flame and terror. She had learned that lesson on one of her first calls as a green-as-grass rookie police officer in Boise, when she was the first one on scene to a deadly house fire on a cold January morning that had killed three children in their sleep.

Wyn rounded the last bend in the road and saw, just as feared, the smoke wasn't coming from a ditch line or a controlled burn of a patch of invading plants. Instead, it twisted sinuously into the sky from the ramshackle barn on Darwin Twitchell's property.

She scanned the area for kids and couldn't see any. What she did see made her blood run cold—two small boys' bikes resting on their sides outside the barn.

Where there were bikes, there were usually boys to ride them.

She parked her vehicle and shoved open her door. "Hello? Anybody here?" she called.

She strained her ears but could hear nothing above the crackle of flames. Heat and flames poured off the building.

She pressed the button on the radio at her shoulder to call dispatch. "I've got a structure fire, an old barn on Darwin Twitchell's property on Conifer Drive, just before Riverbend Road. The upper part seems to be fully engulfed and there's a possibility of civilians inside, juveniles. I've got bikes here but no kids in sight. I'm still looking."

While she raced around the building, she heard the call go out to the volunteer fire department and Chief Gallegos respond that his crews were six minutes out.

"Anybody here?" she called again.

Just faintly, she thought she heard a high cry in response, but her radio crackled with static at that instant and she couldn't be sure. A second later, she heard Cade's voice.

"Bailey, this is Chief Emmett. What's the status of the kids? Over."

She hurried back to her vehicle and popped the trunk. "I can't see them," she answered tersely, digging for a couple of water bottles and an extra T-shirt she kept back there. "I'm going in."

"Negative!" Cade's urgency fairly crackled through the radio. "The first fire crew's ETA is now four minutes. Stand down."

She turned back to the fire and was almost positive the flames seemed to be crackling louder, the smoke billowing higher into the sky. She couldn't stand the thought of children being caught inside that hellish scene. She couldn't. She pushed away the memory of those tiny charred bodies.

Maybe whoever had tripped Darwin's alarms—maybe the same kids who likely set the fire—had run off into the surrounding trees. She hoped so, she really did, but her gut told her otherwise.

In four minutes, they could be burned to a crisp, just like those sweet little kids in Boise. She had to take a look.

It's what her father would have done.

You know what John Wayne would say, John Bailey's voice seemed to echo in her head. *Courage is being scared to death but saddling up anyway.*

Yeah, Dad. I know.

Her hands were sweaty with fear, but she pushed past it and focused on the situation at hand. "I'm going in," she repeated.

"Stand down, Officer Bailey. That is a direct order."

Cade ran a fairly casual—though efficient—police department and rarely pushed rank, but right now he sounded hard, dangerous.

She paused for only a second, her attention caught by sunlight glinting off one of the bikes.

"Wynona, do you copy?" Cade demanded.

She couldn't do it. She couldn't stand out here and wait for the fire department. Time was of the essence, she knew it in her bones. After five years as a police officer, she had learned to rely on her instincts and she couldn't ignore them now.

She was just going to have to disregard his order and deal with his fury later.

"I can't hear you," she lied. "Sorry. You're crackling out."

She squelched her radio to keep him out of her ears, ripped the T-shirt and doused it with her water bottle, then held it to her mouth and pushed inside.

The shift from sunlight to smoke and darkness inside the barn was disorienting. As she had seen from outside, the flames seemed to be limited for now to the upper hayloft of the barn, but the air was thick and acrid.

"Hello?" she called out. "Anybody here?"

"Yes! Help!"

"Please help!"

Two distinct, high, terrified voices came from the far end of the barn.

"Okay. Okay," she called back, her heart pounding fiercely. "Keep talking so I can follow your voice."

There was a momentary pause. "What should we say?"

"Sing a song. How about 'Jingle Bells'? Here. I'll start."

She started the words off and then stopped when she heard two young voices singing the words between sobs. She whispered a quick prayer for help and courage, then rapidly picked her way over rubble and debris as she followed the song to its source, which turned out to be two white-faced, terrified boys she knew.

Caleb and Lucas Keegan were crouched together just below a ladder up to the loft, where the flames sizzled and popped overhead.

Caleb, the older of the two, was stretched out on the ground, his leg bent at an unnatural angle.

"Hey, Caleb. Hey, Luke."

They both sobbed when they spotted her. "Officer Bailey. We didn't mean to start the fire! We didn't mean to!" Luke, the younger one, was close to hysteria, but she didn't have time to calm him.

"We can worry about that later. Right now, we need to get out of here."

"We tried, but Caleb broked his leg! He fell and he can't walk. I was trying to pull him out, but I'm not strong enough."

"I told him to go without me," the older boy, no more than ten, said through tears. "I screamed and screamed at him, but he wouldn't go."

"We're all getting out of here." She ripped the wet cloth in half and handed a section to each boy.

Yeah, she knew the whole adage—taught by the airline industry, anyway—about taking care of yourself before turning your attention to helping others, but this case was worth an exception.

"Caleb, I'm going to pick you up. It's going to hurt, especially if I bump that broken leg of yours, but I don't have time to give you first aid."

"It doesn't matter. I don't care. Do what you have to do. We have to get Luke out of here!"

Her eyes burned from the smoke and her throat felt tight and achy. If she had time to spare, she would have wept at the boy's quiet courage. "I'm sorry," she whispered. She scooped him up into a fireman's carry, finally appreciating the efficiency of the hold. He probably weighed close to eighty pounds, but adrenaline gave her strength.

Over the crackles and crashes overhead, she heard him swallow a scream as his ankle bumped against her.

"Luke, grab hold of my belt buckle, right there in the back. That's it. Do not let go, no matter what. You hear me?"

"Yes," the boy whispered.

"I can't carry you both. I wish I could. You ready?"

"I'm scared," Luke whimpered through the wet T-shirt wrapped around his mouth.

So am I, kiddo. She forced a confident smile she was far from feeling. "Stay close to me. We're tough. We can do this."

The pep talk was meant for herself, more than the boys. Flames had finally begun crawling down the side of the barn and it didn't take long for the fire to slither its way through the old hay and debris scattered through the place.

She did *not* want to run through those flames, but her dad's voice seemed to ring again in her ears.

You never know how strong you are until being strong is the only choice you've got.

Okay, okay. She got it, already.

She ran toward the door, keeping Caleb on her shoulder with one hand while she wrapped her other around Luke's neck.

They were just feet from the door when the younger boy stumbled and went down. She could hear the flames growling louder and knew the dry, rotten barn wood was going to combust any second.

With no time to spare, she half lifted him with her

other arm and dragged them all through the door and into the sunshine while the fire licked and growled at their heels.

* * * * *

Don't miss RIVERBEND ROAD by New York Times
bestselling author RaeAnne Thayne,
available July 2016 wherever HQN books
and ebooks are sold.
www.Harlequin.com

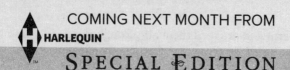

COMING NEXT MONTH FROM

SPECIAL EDITION

Available July 19, 2016

#2491 HER MAVERICK M.D.
Montana Mavericks: The Baby Bonanza • by Teresa Southwick
Nurse Dawn Laramie refuses to fall for a doctor she works with and put her job at risk...*again*! But Jonathon Clifton won't let her cold shoulder get to him. When these two finally bury the hatchet and become friends, will they be able to resist the wild attraction between them?

#2492 AN UNLIKELY DADDY
Conard County: The Next Generation • by Rachel Lee
Pregnant widow Marisa Hayes is still grieving her husband's death when his best friend, Ryker Tremaine, arrives on her doorstep. He promised to watch out for Marisa in case anything happened to Johnny, but the more time he spends with her, the more he longs to help her through her grief for a new life—and love—with him.

#2493 HIS BADGE, HER BABY...THEIR FAMILY?
Men of the West • by Stella Bagwell
Geena and Vince Parcell were married once before, until the stress of Vince's job as a police detective took its toll. Six years later, when Geena shows up in Carson City pregnant and missing her memories, they have a second chance at becoming the family they always wanted.

#2494 A DOG AND A DIAMOND
The McKinnels of Jewell Rock • by Rachael Johns
The closest thing Chelsea Porter has to a family is her beloved dog. When she attends the McKinnel family Thanksgiving with Callum McKinnel, she finds the love and warmth she's always craved. Can they work through their fears from the past to make a future together?

#2495 ALWAYS THE BEST MAN
Crimson, Colorado • by Michelle Major
After a nasty divorce, Emily Whittaker is back in Crimson with her son. Jase Crenshaw thought he was over his high school crush on Emily, but when they team up as best man and maid of honor for her brother's wedding, Jase thinks he's finally found his chance to win the girl of his dreams...

#2496 THE DOCTOR'S RUNAWAY FIANCÉE
Rx for Love • by Cindy Kirk
When Sylvie Thorne broke their engagement, Dr. Andrew O'Shea realized he didn't know the woman he loved at all. So when he finds out she's in Wyoming, he decides to get some answers. Sylvie still thinks she made the right decision, but when Andrew moves in to get closure, she's not sure she'll be able to resist the man he becomes away from his high-society family.

YOU CAN FIND MORE INFORMATION ON UPCOMING HARLEQUIN® TITLES, FREE EXCERPTS AND MORE AT WWW.HARLEQUIN.COM.

HSECNM0716

SPECIAL EXCERPT FROM

 HARLEQUIN

SPECIAL EDITION

*Can secret agent Ryker Tremaine help his best friend's
pregnant widow, Marisa Hayes, overcome her grief
and make a new life—and love—with him?*

*Read on for a sneak preview of
AN UNLIKELY DADDY,
the next book in* New York Times *bestselling author
Rachel Lee's long-running miniseries*
CONARD COUNTY: THE NEXT GENERATION.

"Am I awful?"

"Awful? What in the world would make you think that?"

"Because…because…" She put her face in her hands.

At once Ryker squatted beside her, worried, touching her
arm. "Marisa? What's wrong?"

"Nothing. It's just… I shouldn't be having these feelings."

"What feelings?" Suicidal thoughts? Urges to kill
someone? Fear? The whole palette of emotions lay there
waiting for her to choose one.

She kept her face covered. "I have dreams about you."

His entire body leaped. He had dreams about her, too, and
not only when he was sleeping. "And?"

"I want you. Is that wrong? I mean…it hasn't been that
long…"

Her words deprived him of breath. He could have lifted
her right then and carried her to her bed. He'd have done
so joyfully. But caution and maybe even some wisdom held
him back.

"I want you, too," he said huskily.

She dropped her hands, her wondering eyes meeting his almost shyly. "Really? Looking like this?"

"You're beautiful looking just like that. But…"

"But?" She seized on the word, some of the wonder leaving her face.

"I don't want you to regret it. So how about we spend more time talking to each other? Give yourself some time to be sure. Hell, it probably wouldn't be safe anyway."

"My doc says it would."

She'd asked her doctor? A thousand explosions went off in his head, leaving him almost blind. He cleared his throat. "Uh…I could take you right now. I want to. So, please, don't be embarrassed. I don't think you're awful. But…please… get to know me a bit better. I want to know you better. I want you to be sure."

"I feel guilty," she admitted. "It's been driving me nuts. Am I betraying Johnny?"

"I don't believe he'd think so. But that's a question only you can answer, and you need to do that for yourself. Then there's me."

"You?" She studied him.

"I don't exactly feel right about this. After what you've already been through, I shouldn't have to explain that. I'm just like John, Marisa. Why in the world would you want to risk that again?"

She nodded slowly, looking down at where her fingertips pressed into the wooden table. "I don't know," she finally said quietly.

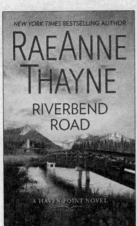

NEW YORK TIMES BESTSELLING AUTHOR

RaeAnne Thayne

RIVERBEND ROAD

A HAVEN POINT NOVEL

$7.99 U.S./$9.99 CAN.

EXCLUSIVE
Limited Time Offer

$1.⁰⁰ OFF

Return to Haven Point, where
New York Times *bestselling author*

RaeAnne Thayne

proves there's no sweeter place
to fall in love...

RIVERBEND ROAD

Available June 21, 2016.
Pick up your copy today!

HQN™

- ✂

$1.⁰⁰ OFF   the purchase price of RIVERBEND ROAD by RaeAnne Thayne.

Offer valid from June 21, 2016, to July 31, 2016. Redeemable at participating
retail outlets. Not redeemable at Barnes & Noble.
Limit one coupon per purchase. Valid in the U.S.A. and Canada only.

52614053

5 65373 00076 2   (8100)0 12196

PHCOUPRAT0716

THE WORLD IS BETTER WITH

Romance

Harlequin has everything from contemporary, passionate and heartwarming to suspenseful and inspirational stories.

Whatever your mood, we have a romance just for you!

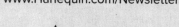